SOLD TO THE BERSERKERS

A MENAGE SHIFTER ROMANCE

LEE SAVINO

SIGN UP TO LEE'S NEWSLETTER AT LEESAVINO.COM

FREE BOOK

Get a secret Berserker book, Bred by the Berserkers (only to the awesomesauce fans on Lee's email list)
Go here to get started... https://geni.us/BredBerserker

1

The day my stepfather sold me to the Berserkers, I woke at dawn with him leering over me. "Get up." He made to kick me and I scrambled out of my sleep stupor to my feet.

"I need your help with a delivery."

I nodded and glanced at my sleeping mother and siblings. I didn't trust my stepfather around my three younger sisters, but if I was gone with him all day, they'd be safe. I'd taken to carrying a dirk myself. I did not dare kill him; we needed him for food and shelter, but if he attacked me again, I would fight.

My mother's second husband hated me, ever since the last time he'd tried to take me and I had fought back. My mother was gone to market, and when he tried to grab me, something in me snapped. I would not let him touch me again. I fought, kicking and scratching, and finally grabbing an iron pot and scalding him with heated water.

He bellowed and looked as if he wanted to hurt me, but kept his distance. When my mother returned he pretended like nothing was wrong, but his eyes followed me with hatred and cunning.

Out loud he called me ugly and mocking the scar that marred my neck since a wild dog attacked me when I was young. I ignored this and kept my distance. I'd heard the taunts about my hideous face since the wounds had healed into scars, a mass of silver tissue at my neck.

That morning, I wrapped a scarf over my hair and scarred neck and followed my stepfather, carrying his wares down the old road. At first I thought we were headed to the great market, but when we reached the fork in the road and he went an unfamiliar way, I hesitated. Something wasn't right.

"This way, cur." He'd taken to calling me "dog". He'd taunted me, saying the only sounds I could make were grunts like a beast, so I might as well be one. He was right. The attack had taken my voice by damaging my throat.

If I followed him into the forest and he tried to kill me, I wouldn't even be able to cry out.

"There's a rich man who asked for his wares delivered to his door." He marched on without a backward glance and I followed.

I had lived all my life in the kingdom of Alba, but when my father died and my mother remarried, we moved to my stepfather's village in the highlands, at the foot of the great, forbidding mountains. There were stories of evil that lived in the dark crevices of the heights, but I'd never believed them.

I knew enough monsters living in plain sight.

The longer we walked, the lower the sun sank in the sky, the more I knew my stepfather was trying to trick me, that there was no rich man waiting for these wares.

When the path curved, and my stepfather stepped out

from behind a boulder to surprise me, I was half ready, but before I could reach for my dirk he struck me so hard I fell.

I woke tied to a tree.

The light was lower, heralding dusk. I struggled silently, frantic gasps escaping from my scarred throat. My stepfather stepped into view and I felt a second of relief at a familiar face, before remembering the evil this man had wrought on my body. Whatever he was planning, it would bode ill for me, and my younger sisters. If I didn't survive, they would eventually share the same fate as mine.

"You're awake," he said. "Just in time for the sale."

I strained but my bonds held fast. As my stepfather approached, I realized that the scarf that I wrapped around my neck to hide my scars had fallen, exposing them. Out of habit, I twitched my head to the side, tucking my bad side towards my shoulder.

My stepfather smirked.

"So ugly," he sneered. "I could never find a husband for you, but I found someone to take you. A group of warriors passing through who saw you, and want to slake their lust on your body. Who knows, if you please them, they may let you live. But I doubt you'll survive these men. They're foreigners, mercenaries, come to fight for the king. Berserkers. If you're lucky your death will be swift when they tear you apart."

I'd heard the tales of berserker warriors, fearsome warriors of old. Ageless, timeless, they'd sailed over the seas to the land, plundering, killing, taking slaves, they fought for our kings, and their own. Nothing could stand in their path when they went into a killing rage.

I fought to keep my fear off my face. Berserkers were a myth, so my stepfather had probably sold me to a band of passing soldiers who would take their pleasure from my flesh before leaving me for dead, or selling me on.

"I could've sold you long ago, if I stripped you bare and put a bag over you head to hide those scars."

His hands pawed at me, and I shied away from his disgusting breath. He slapped me, then tore at my braid, letting my hair spill over my face and shoulders.

Bound as I was, I still could glare at him. I could do nothing to stop the sale, but I hoped my fierce expression told him I'd fight to the death if he tried to force himself on me.

His hand started to wander down towards my breast when a shadow moved on the edge of the clearing. It caught my eye and I startled. My stepfather stepped back as the warriors poured from the trees.

My first thought was that they were not men, but beasts. They prowled forward, dark shapes almost one with the shadows. A few wore animal pelts and held back, lurking on the edge of the woods. Two came forward, wearing the garb of warriors, bristling with weapons. One had dark hair, and the other long, dirty blond with a beard to match.

Their eyes glowed with a terrifying light.

As they approached, the smell of raw meat and blood wafted over us, and my stomach twisted. I was glad my stepfather hadn't fed me all day, or I would've emptied my guts on the ground.

My stepfather's face and tone took on the wheedling expression I'd seen when he was selling in the market.

"Good evening, sirs," he cringed before the largest, the blond with hair streaming down his chest.

They were perfectly silent, but the blond approached, fixing me with strange golden eyes.

Their faces were fair enough, but their hulking forms

and the quick, light way they moved made me catch my breath. I had never seen such massive men. Beside them, my stepfather looked like an ugly dwarf.

"This is the one you wanted," my stepfather continued. "She's healthy and strong. She will be a good slave for you."

My body would've shaken with terror, if I were not bound so tightly.

A dark haired warrior stepped up beside the blond and the two exchanged a look.

"You asked for the one with scars." My stepfather took my hair and jerked my head back, exposing the horrible, silvery mass. I shut my eyes, tears squeezing out at the sudden pain and humiliation.

The next thing I knew, my stepfather's grip loosened. A grunt, and I opened my eyes to see the dark haired warrior standing at my side. My stepfather sprawled on the ground as if he'd been pushed.

The blond leader prodded a boot into my stepfather's side.

"Get up," the blond said, in a voice that was more a growl than a human sound. It curdled my blood. My stepfather scrambled to his feet.

The black haired man cut away the last of my bonds, and I sagged forward. I would've fallen but he caught me easily and set me on my feet, keeping his arms around me. I was not the smallest woman, but he was a giant. Muscles bulged in his arms and chest, but he held me carefully. I stared at him, taking in his raven dark hair and strange gold eyes.

He tucked me closer to his muscled body.

Meanwhile, my stepfather whined. "I just wanted to show you the scars—"

Again that frightening growl from the blond. "You don't touch what is ours."

"I don't want to touch her." My stepfather spat.

Despite myself, I cowered against the man who held me. A stranger I had never met, he was still a safer haven than my stepfather.

"I only wish to make sure you are satisfied, milords. Do you want to sample her?" my stepfather asked in an evil tone. He wanted to see me torn apart.

A growl rumbled under my ear and I lifted my head. Who were these men, these great warriors who had bought and paid for me? The arms around my body were strong and solid, inescapable, but the gold eyes looking down at me were kind. The warrior ran his thumb across the pad of my lips, and his fingers were gentle for such a large, violent looking warrior. Under the scent of blood, he smelled of snow and sharp cold, a clean scent.

He pressed his face against my head, breathing in a deep breath.

The blond was looking at us.

"It's her," the black haired man growled, his voice so guttural. "This is the one."

One of his hands came to cover the side of my face and throat, holding my face to his chest in a protective gesture.

I closed my eyes, relaxing in the solid warmth of the warrior's body.

A clink of gold, and the deed was done. I'd been sold.

⁓

Almost immediately, the warrior started pulling me away.

I fought my rising panic, wishing that my stepfather's was not the last familiar face I saw.

"Goodbye, Brenna," my stepfather smirked as the warriors streamed past him, following their blond leader into the forest.

"Wait," the blond stopped. Immediately the warriors grabbed my stepfather. "Her name is Brenna?"

"Yes. But you bought her. Call her what you like."

The dark haired warrior tugged me on. I half followed, half staggered along beside him. My nails bit into my palms so I could keep myself from panicking. Fighting the giant beside me wasn't an option. Neither was trying to outrun him.

The blond joined us, and the two warriors pulled me into the dark grove. Terrible thoughts poured into my mind. I belonged to these men, and now they would rape me, sate themselves with my body, then cut my throat and leave me for the wolves.

My eyes filled with tears, both angry and frightened.

They stopped as one and drew me between them. I shut my eyes in defiance, and the tears leaked out.

As I healed from the attack, I could make some noises, horrible, animal things, but they were so ugly, I stopped making any sounds at all. Sometimes, when alone, I'd sink into the river, open my mouth and try to scream. But no sound came out anymore. My throat had forgotten my voice.

Now the only sound in the grove was my harsh breathing.

I sensed the warriors on either side of me, their massive shapes towering over my fragile body. I was much smaller than them, tiny and petite beside their massive forms.

Right now I tried to remember to breathe and submit to these men. One blow and they could kill me.

My heart beat so hard it was painful. I was ready to die.

But when they touched me they were gentle. A hand

brushed back my hair, then stroked my jaw. One steadied me from behind as the other cupped my head and turned my head this way and that. The one behind me gathered my hair behind me. I held my breath as the two massive warriors handled me.

I realized the smell of blood had fallen away, replaced by another scent, an animal musk that was much more pleasant.

A finger ran over my neck, near the scar and I sucked in a breath. The hands dropped away.

Their faces dipped close to mine, and I felt their breath on my skin as if they took deep scents of my hair.

"So good," one of them groaned.

I didn't understand. I was afraid of them taking me but I didn't know why they weren't.

"It's working," one murmured to the other. "The witch was right."

As they dipped their heads and scented me, my heart beat faster in response to their proximity. Something stirred deep inside me. Desire. A few minutes alone with these men and I'd been more intimate with them than any other.

As one they bent their heads to mine, nuzzling close to my neck a tingling spread over my skin.

I felt it then, unbidden, a stirring in my loins. Ever since I had come into womanhood, my desires were strong. Every month I fought the pull to find a man and join with him. I was hideous and destined to be an outcast and alone. But each full moon my body came alive, beset by waves of roiling lust until I felt desperate enough to grab the nearest man and beg him to give me sons.

The heat poured over me until I heard a gasp—one of the warriors jerked back and stepped away.

"She's ready," one growled. Instead of frightening, the sound excited me.

What was happening?

"Not here, brother," the blond rasped.

Without answering, the dark-haired one pulled me on.

For a while we walked, pushing through the forest and forded a stream. The heat in me faded as I followed, weak with hunger and fear, eventually stumbling on exhaustion numbed feet.

The dark-haired warrior stopped, and I flinched, expecting him to bully me into continuing on.

Instead, he guided me to face him. Again his hands came to me, stroking back my hair. I winced when I realized what he was doing: looking at my scar.

Involuntarily my head jerked and he let my chin go, offering me water instead. He held the skin while I drank, and when I'd had my fill he offered me dried meat, feeding me from his hand. I stared into the strange golden eyes, unable to keep the questions off my face: Who are you? What are you going to do with me?

When I was done, he lay a hand on his chest and uttered a guttural sound I didn't understand. He repeated it twice, then lay his hand on my chest.

"Brenna." I could barely make out my name, but I nodded.

A shadow of a smile curved his full lips. Shrugging off the gray pelt he wore, he wrapped it around my shoulders before pulling me back into the circle of his strong arms.

My heart beat faster. The pelt's warmth seeped into my tired body, and the big man held me steady. I still felt frightened, but waited obediently in the dark haired warrior's embrace. I dared not struggle.

The brush around us rippled and the warriors

surrounded us. I shrank towards my black-haired captor, but he held me fast, turning me so I faced the warrior who seemed to be their leader.

The blond was so huge, my neck had to tip back to see him. He moved forward and I couldn't help trembling so hard I would've fallen if the dark haired warrior let me go. Every instinct in me screamed that this was a wild man, a beast a dangerous monster and I needed to run.

He reached out and I flinched.

His hand halted.

He swallowed, as if trying to remember how to use his voice.

"Brenna." My name was no more than a soft growl. "We mean you no harm."

I studied him. As big as the warriors were, the blond was one of the largest. He walked lightly, muscles bulging. Long locks of blond hair brushed his broad shoulders. His face was rawboned and half covered in a beard, the defining feature his great gold eyebrows over those amazing eyes.

When his gaze caught mine, his eyes glowed.

His hands touched my face, a thumb stroking my lips. He tilted it to and fro. He pushed my hair away from my neck. I shut my eyes, knowing what he saw, the white weals and gnarled tissue, healed into a disfiguring scar that had taken my voice, and nearly taken my life.

I barely remembered the attack: a large dark shape rushing at me from the shadows, then pain. Lots of pain. My mother told me I lay near death for days. No one thought I would survive, but I did.

Some believed it would be better if I hadn't. Even though I healed from the attack, the scars marked my face and my life. The boys used to chase me down the street, throwing things. I grew up learning to blend into the shadows. To move silently so I wouldn't draw attention to myself. Later, when my mother married my stepfather, I learned to cower and hide.

Her body is pretty enough, my stepfather had said. *Just put a bag over her head so you can stand it.*

Now my new owner tipped my head this way and that, studying the scar. He nodded, looking satisfied. "The mark of the wolf," he rasped.

A ripple went around the assembled men, and the other warriors pressed closer. The black haired man held me still, hefty arms around my body.

I wished I could ask what the blond warrior meant.

The men surrounded me, staring at my hideous scars.

My blond captor released my jaw and I ducked my head down again in shame. His large, rough hands caught my head again, and raised it, but this time he cupped my face.

I shut my eyes. I couldn't even cry out. This man now owned me. I'd resigned myself to living life with a disfigured face, unwanted and unloved, but I'd never thought I'd become a slave.

"Brenna," The command came in that rasping growl. "Look at me."

Somehow I obeyed and met the leader's steady gaze. Something in that golden glow mesmerized me, and I felt calmer.

"Do not be afraid." His throat worked for a moment, as if he was trying to remember how to speak. "Is it true you cannot speak?"

I nodded.

"Can you read or write?"

I shook my head. This was the strangest conversation I'd had in my nineteen years.

He looked frustrated, exchanging glances with the warrior who held me.

A voice spoke at my ear, still rough and guttural, but a bit more clearly than before. "We would like to find a way to talk to ye." The speaker turned me to face him, and I flinched as he brought his hand up, but he only examined the scars as the blond had.

By the time he was done, all warriors but the blond had melted away. Dark hair touched my cheek and I winced, realizing there was a bruise on my face from when my stepfather struck me.

The blond crowded closer, a sound rumbling in his great chest, not unlike a growl.

"Brenna," he said. "We will not hurt you. I swear it. No one will ever hurt you again."

The dark haired one took a few locks of my hair in his hand, gripping them lightly and raising them to his face. He breathed in my scent, then looked at me with glowing eyes and said in a clear voice.

"Ye belong to us now."

∼

The rest of the night passed in a blur. We walked into the woods, the thick darkness, and went along a path. The warriors went behind and before, I was safe in the middle.

Finally exhaustion took over and I stumbled. Instantly, the dark haired warrior swung me up in his arms, and the group's pace increased. His hand came up, pressing my face to his neck.

I must have slept, for when I woke again, the blond was carrying me. I lifted my head blinking in the starlight and cold night air. The warriors must have walked all night, and were still hiking, following a trail up a mountain. I roused a little and stared into the leader's golden eyes.

"Sleep," he grunted. "Almost home."

~

I DO NOT KNOW how long I slept, but as I slept I dreamed. The starlight fell away into a deeper darkness. I was in a warm, safe place with two warriors leaning over me, large hands sifting through my hair. One of them pulled out a dirk and sliced away my gown, and then the hands began stroking down my body. Their touches fed my heated desire, and in my dream I longed to pull their bodies over mine, wordlessly begging them to fill me.

Instead, I lay still as they touched me with reverent fingers. I heard them speak, but not out loud. They didn't use words but somehow I understood them.

"The witch was right. She calms the wolf."

A grunt of agreement, then a pause. "I can smell her heat."

"Patience, brother. We have waited this long."

They lay on either side of me, still touching me. In the darkness their eyes glowed.

"Brother," one said in a tone of awe. "The beast rests."

"As does mine."

"It has been so long."

"Too long. But the struggle is over. The beast will sleep again."

2

I woke cradled in softness, my body a bit too warm. Sweat trickled down my bare breasts. My gown was gone; the memory of the warriors stripping me, at least, wasn't a dream.

When I moved, I touched a body lying in front of me and my eyes flew open. A warrior lay beside me, his large form in repose. We rested in a pile of pelts, in a dark room lit by a fire. In my sleep, I'd curled on my side facing the dark haired warrior and there was barely a hairsbreath between my bare chest and his.

Stretching a little, I pushed the thick fur from me.

His body felt so warm. I wriggled back a little, and the man's eyes opened and twinkled. I met his gaze without fear. We'd shared only a night and half a day, but I felt at ease with his friendly expression. His smile boded well for my life as a slave.

"Brenna," he greeted me, and his voice, rough with sleep, sounded clearer to my ears. "Did ye sleep well?"

I nodded. He rolled onto his side, facing me, and his broad, muscled chest filled my vision. Part of me wanted to cringe and slip away, but I reminded myself that this was my new master. I may as well lay there and let him do what he would. Besides, I was comfortable on the pelts.

The warrior shifted closer, his light brown eyes glowing brighter. I could make out every dark lash. Slowly, as if he might startle me, he lifted a large rough hand, and touched my face with more care than I would've guessed he could muster. I lowered my eyes as he caressed me, letting him take liberties, smoothing my skin and pushing back my hair.

Strange as it was, lying beside a man I'd never met, one who'd bought me in the woods in a humiliating transaction, I enjoyed the moment, the warrior's rough and gentle fingers. An outcast who kept to her accepted lot, I wasn't often touched. It felt nice.

Too late I realized he was exploring my scar and jerked my head away.

"Shhh, still. I won't hurt you."

My hand came up to cover the scarred side of my neck and face.

He gazed at me with honest eyes. "You don't like it?"

I shook my head. The scar was my bane, my curse. It made me too ugly for marriage to a village boy, made me fit only to be a slave.

My hand pressed harder, but he took it and pulled it off my face, frowning a little as he examined the weals underneath. As much as I wanted to struggle, I held my body still. This was not my secret lover, or a friend. He was a warrior who had bought and paid for me. I had to remember that, if I was to survive.

My new life's aim was pleasing my new masters. The longer I did that, and stayed alive, the higher my chances to one day find a way to escape.

I held onto this thought as I stared at my dark haired bedmate, blinking hard to hold back tears.

"Isnae so bad, lass. Just a wee mark. It makes ye different, but it isnae enough to take from yer beauty."

I blinked. No one had ever called me beautiful. The warrior pulled my hand away from my face and kissed it. His lips worked at my palm, tickling me with the bristles on his chin and jaw. The skin around his eyes crinkled with a mischievous smile.

Just like that, I felt warmth rush to all my secret parts. My womb clenched and filled with longing.

The flood of desire was so sudden and shocking, I automatically tried to tug my hand away.

He didn't let it go. Turning my hand, he laid kisses down my wrist, sucking lightly at the skin over my pulse. My heartbeat leapt tellingly, and he grinned full on.

"That's it, Brenna. There's a good lass." His eyes caught fire, brightening with that otherworldly glow.

Despite myself, I shifted, feeling arousal pool as wetness between my legs.

He paused, scenting the air. If I'd thought his eyes were golden before, they burned ten times hotter when he angled his head closer to me. Slowly he bent his head, ready to touch his mouth to mine... Transfixed by those beautiful eyes, I couldn't move if I tried.

Something moved behind me and I startled, then panicked. I caught a glimpse of blond locks as I started thrashing. There was another man in the bed. In my fixation on the dark-haired warrior, I hadn't noticed the second, massive form.

Before I could rise, the dark haired one caught me, pulling my trembling body back onto the pelts.

"Be still," another voice rumbled.

Immediately I froze. The animal sound raised the hairs on the back of my head.

The dark haired man wrapped burly arms around my torso. His thigh rested over my legs, capturing me thoroughly. "Calm, lass," he breathed into my ear. "Tis only Samuel."

Slowly I turned my head to Samuel and met the warrior's wild gaze.

"Do ye remember Samuel? He carried ye up the mountain. Dinnae hurt his feelings. He will grow surly and sulk all day."

My brow furrowed until I realized they were teasing me. Under the short beard, Samuel's mouth softened a little from its serious expression.

"Starting without me, Daegan?" he spoke over my head to his warrior brother.

"Just a wee kiss." The black haired warrior rolled me to my back so I could look up at both of them. I swallowed hard, trying not to show on my face how intimidated I was.

They loomed over me, one dark and the other fair. One serious and intense, the other with a mischievous glinting light in his eye.

Their touches became bolder. One hand soothed down my hip.

The worst was how my body responded. I shifted anxiously as a prickle of heat curled through me. I fought it, closing my eyes.

"Open." One of the warriors grunted, smoothing my hair back from my face.

I did and he rewarded me, bending down as if to kiss me. He inhaled deeply, then raised his head.

"So good," he commented to his brother.

"Just as the witch said." Samuel ran a long finger down the side of my face.

"Do ye feel it?"

"I feel it," the blond confirmed. Their voices were still rough and deep but they were stronger.

The dark haired warrior reared over me, settling beside me as I lay back looking up at him.

"Brenna," he said, putting his hand on my chest as he had last night. His voice was much clearer than the guttural grunt it had been before. He placed his hand on his chest, and this time I caught his name. "Daegan."

He seemed to be waiting for me to answer, so I nodded.

"Samuel," the other said.

Like my dream last night, their hands started stroking up and down my body. Starting with my face and drifting down either arm, their hands touched and caressed.

Samuel's brushed my breast, my nipple hardened suddenly and I startled.

"Shhh, relax," the blond said. "It's all right."

"So lovely," Daegan added, running a single finger down my arm, sending shivers through my entire body. "Do ye like our touch, lass?"

I blinked at him, afraid to nod or shake my head. A part of me liked it, and a part of me knew I shouldn't. It was all happening so fast.

"You're ours now, Brenna. We bought you because we wished for a woman to share our bed. We believe you are the one," Samuel said.

"Obey us, lass, and we'll cherish and protect you, and give you pleasure."

I lay stiff, trying to wrap my head around their words. The events of the past night and day still jumbled in my head.

Daegan wrapped his hand around my ankle and I had to force myself not to kick. It was his ankle now, to caress or crush as he pleased. I was their slave.

Fear must have tracked across my face, for Samuel spoke in a soothing tone. "Calm Brenna, give yourself over to us. We have long awaited you."

I blinked. They'd awaited me?

The big leader stroked my cheek. "We own you now, and we will care for you and protect you. You will never come to any harm."

His thumb went to my lip and ran over the soft skin there. My heart beat faster, but not only with fear.

He sighed. "I wish you could speak to us. I would give anything to know your questions. Take away the fear in your eyes."

I tried to relax. These men had bought me but then now sought to comfort.

Samuel shifted over me and pinned me with that intense gaze. Daegan positioned himself at my head, cradling it in the crook of his arm and playing with my hair.

"We will see to ye now." Samuel reared over me and pulled the pelt away from my body. I couldn't move as if I'd turned to stone with fear. I lay naked before these great warriors, who feasted on my flesh with a golden gaze.

"Lovely," Daegan said, and I went from afraid to excited in a few seconds.

Samuel bent so his hair brushed my upper thighs and bent his head. He seemed to be scenting me.

I tried to close my legs and he held them open. Daegan lifted me so he could hold me half in his lap, my head against his chest. He reached down and laid palms on my thighs to keep them apart for his warrior brother.

Feeling trapped, I started struggling. Despite their kind

words, I didn't know these men or what they would do with me.

"Brenna," Samuel turned my name into a command. "Lie still. We will not hurt you. You are our most treasured possession."

Daegan stroked my inner thigh. "Ye dinnae ken now, but you will."

Samuel brushed fingers over my center. "This belongs to us now." He moved his hands a little and my hips shifted of their own volition, responding.

If I could've cried out or made a little noise of longing, I would've.

All too soon, he took his fingers away, smelling my musk, then tasting it.

My own mouth parted in a gasp, and it proved too much for Daegan. One hand left my thighs and gripped my hair gently, turning it so he could kiss me. His lips touched mine, pecking and inviting before his head slanted and he drank more deeply of my mouth. I stilled with shock at my first kiss.

He pulled away with a mischievous light in his eye. "Do ye like that?" His brow went up, almost daring me to say no.

I just stared.

Samuel almost grinned.

"Let me try again." Daegan did grin, full out before he bent and teased at my lips with his tongue. Heat flared through me.

"My turn," Samuel leaned forward. Daegan cradled me as the big man cupped my face, drawing me forward with tender fingers before touching his lips to mine. Like his warrior brother, he tasted of clean and good, and when my lips parted, his tongue slipped inside.

By the time the kiss ended, I was breathing hard. Wet heat pooled at my center.

Samuel took his time, kissing me again, then offering my mouth back to Daegan. Their hands moved over my skin nonstop, stroking my arms, breasts, hips and waist and down my legs. Between four hands and twin mouths, they left no part of me uncaressed....except one.

After a time my legs lay open of their own accord, my center exposed and begging for attention.

The heat rose in me stronger than ever before, the fire fed by the readying touches of two men. I fought it as I always had, struggling to remain myself, to hold onto Brenna. Each kiss, each touch, each swipe of tongue at my neck or knee and I lost myself a little bit more.

Samuel drew back for a moment and I blinked at the respite. His long hair streamed over an awesome chest. Daegan had a smaller build, though not by much. Every movement displayed muscles on muscles, lean and chiseled.

These were hard men, with hard lives, and I was to lie with both of them.

They marveled at my softness, commenting as they stroked me.

"So smooth. Feel this."

Hands cupped my breast and I arched my back, my breath coming faster as I wordlessly asked for more.

"Such a beautiful lass. So perfect for us."

Samuel's large hands traced down the curve of my hip.

"Perfection." Samuel's fingers brushed between my legs, the barest of touches. "Relax, sweet one, we will now give you pleasure."

At his words, my body convulsed.

"Should we tie her?"

Daegan cuddled me closer. "Do we need to tie you, lass?

I know ye are new and scared, but we own ye now. We will do with your body as we wish, and always care for it. Right now Samuel will give ye pleasure."

"Will you submit to us, Brenna?"

I nodded. What choice did I have?

The big man's touches circled close to my special places and arousal I'd never felt before shot through me. I became a creature empty of all but wanting.

It frightened me. Samuel paused as my panicked hands caught at his.

Daegan caught my wrists and then I jerked against him, panicking straight out. "Breathe, Brenna. My warrior brother is going to give ye pleasure. You cannae fight it. Just relax and give yourself to us."

Hands holding my legs open, Samuel lay down between them. I felt hot breath between my legs. First kisses up my knee then a tongue touching my center. Touching turned to licking. It felt so good I couldn't fight the iron arms holding me. Nor did I want to. Desire and fear warred in me and desire won.

Daegan praised me as I relaxed. "Good lass. Ye were made for this."

"You were born and marked for us, and we have waited so long." Samuel added, then nibbled the inside of my thighs, drawing closer to my weeping slit. By the time his mouth arrived at its destination, I was wet and ready for him.

I knew a little of lovemaking, having seen couples in the woods or guessed from crude jokes I'd heard. Then there were the violent encounters with my stepfather before I determined to fight back.

But I had never experienced such care and gentleness at

the hands of a man, much less two warriors who could kill me as quickly as caress me.

While Daegan's fingers circled my nipples, his mouth kissed my neck and shoulders. His lips slid over my scar but I didn't care any more.

Samuel found my lower lips and flicked his tongue at them, my arousal shot to the sky. My breathing changed, became languid and ready.

A small part of me fought my growing arousal, trying to keep my wits about me. Two men held me in their bed, feasting with delight on my body.

Need pressed through me, the heat that claimed me each month since I became woman with my first bleeding. During full moon my breasts grew heavy and my whole body ached...not with pain, but a pleasurable longing. If I did not control it, I would want to go out and rut like an animal, like a dog my stepfather named me.

I couldn't let it happen, but now two men were tempting me.

"Let go, wee one. Give us your pleasure," Daegan whispered in the rough voice. Their lips, tongues and fingers were insistent, non stop. I felt myself start to crest on the precipice.

I panted as I shattered. Pleasure flooded through my world, taking me higher and higher, beyond feeling.

As I came down I realized the one crying out was me. In my pleasure my throat had opened and sounds had come out. Guttural, awful sounds. The sounds of a beast.

I shut my eyes tight, ashamed. Losing control was more humiliating than being scarred for life, being sold by my hated stepfather, than letting two men pleasure me. I had to remember who I was. I had to stay alert so I could escape. My sisters were counting on me.

"Open your eyes, Brenna." Samuel commanded.

The two men looked pleased with themselves.

The blond's finger brushed my cheek, lifting off a tear, and he frowned.

"Oh, little lass." Daegan tucked close, his hair streaming over my naked body. "You're all right. You're safe here."

"It's a lot to take in," Samuel said. "But we've been waiting for you for a long, long time."

3

After my orgasm, Samuel disappeared from the room with the pelt covered dais. Daegan helped me to my feet and led me, still naked but for my unbound hair, out of the stone cavern, down a hall to another cave.

There was light in the cavern from lit braziers and fire, The hall had some sort of natural light, I hurried with Daegan, the rock cool on my feet.

We were inside a mountain. Someone must have carved this place from the rock. I'd heard of dwarves in the hills, but thought they were also a myth.

My breasts were hard and my body shivering when we stepped into another room. And warm steamy air embraced my body. We were in another cavern, where hot water bubbled out of the rock.

Daegan gave me a grin. "Do ye like it, lass?"

I jerked a nod, wide eyed. As a barely tolerated outcast, I often secluded myself in the forest, bathing in a woodland stream. My clean habits marked me as strange.

It seemed these warriors also appreciated a bath.

At his encouragement, I went into the water, letting the warm water lap around my legs. At its deepest the pool went to my waist. Daegan let me play in the warmth, splashing and lying back so the water covered me up to the neck.

I closed my eyes and pretended I was home, or in some fine luxurious place, a princess with not a care in the world.

A splashing sound brought me to my feet. Daegan waded into the water, naked body cutting through the water in a straight line towards me. The heat in his eye made me blush.

I ducked my chin down to hide my neck and covered my chest with my arms. Outside of my scars, I knew my face and form were pleasing. When they tired of throwing rocks and calling me names, the boys in the village used to try to find me when I was bathing. I learned to hide, especially when the heat filled me. During those times of deep desire, I admired the firm, unblemished skin of my belly and breasts, the curve of my bottom and strong legs. Alone, in desire's thrall, I felt beautiful.

I'd felt that way on the bed between the warriors, a thousand fold.

The sight of the approaching warrior, excited and fierce, with water streaming from his hard, muscled form, made me suddenly shy. My heart beat faster, and I turned my back, pretending to explore the cave. As I expected, his hand stroked down my back, reminding me how little I'd been touched in my lifetime. Until now.

He turned me to face him.

"Are ye hungry?"

I shook my head.

"I am." He pulled me into his arms and slanted his head down, feeding on my lips, nibbling gently before parting them and sweeping his tongue inside. His body pressed against mine, and the heat claimed me again as his kiss and closeness swept my control away. If my light brown eyes could glow as theirs did, they would be hot and bright with desire.

When he broke the kiss, I clung to him, arms twined around his neck so he could not get away.

"Oh, lass." He groaned and pressed his face into my neck. He seemed to breathe in my scent as if I was a source of air.

A noise and we both raised our heads. Samuel stood on the edge of the water, golden eyes glowing, his massive form naked but for a loin cloth.

"Do you see my warrior brother?" Daegan whispered. "He is waiting for you to invite him to join us."

I gripped Daegan's arms.

"We both need ye, little lass," he breathed. "Do ye want him to come too?"

My master wanted me to agree to something. I nodded.

Samuel unslung his loin cloth and I caught a glimpse of his massive rod before he entered the water. Daegan's member poked my buttocks, hard and ready.

Something in me broke, like a bowstring suddenly unstrung.

I wriggled backwards in Daegan's arms, knowing I couldn't escape but having to try. He set me away from him just as Samuel stopped at my side. Both men's arms corralled me loosely.

"Do ye desire us, wee one?"

I swallowed hard.

"She is afraid." Samuel said.

"No matter. She is ours now."

Daegan's hands skimmed up my sides, cupping my breasts, smoothing over them. Despite myself, I relaxed into his touch, even as I stared into Samuel' golden gaze. His eyes were so bright.

Daegan's hands slid down securing my hips. Samuel came and bent and kissed me. It was too much, Daegan's hands stroking up and down my torso, Samuel's hands on my face, mouth on mine, drinking me down.

Arousal poured over me like fire. Samuel's hands went down to my legs, Daegan grasped my hips and the two men lifted me.

"We will take ye now," Daegan whispered. "You will know yer pleasure, and ours." My head lolled back onto Daegan's chest as Samuel set himself against my wet center.

His member rubbed up and down, I closed my eyes, feeling every part of me clench.

He let my legs down. "Not here," he told his warrior brother.

Daegan handed me to Samuel and the blond lifted me, carrying me quickly back to the room with the pelts. My arms went around his neck, fixated on his golden eyes.

"Calm, little love," he whispered to me. "There's no need to fear." He set me down on the pelts and eased me back. "We will make sure you find your pleasure."

Again the soft touches up and down my legs, coaxing me open. This time I let my head sag back and my mind drift away to enjoy the hands massaging my skin.

"Beautiful," someone said near my head and I opened my eyes. Daegan leaned over me, kissing me. He tasted sweet.

Meanwhile Samuel kissed up my leg to my soft lower lips, finding and lapping at my pleasure bud. With one warrior above and one below, dominating and claiming, my orgasm rolled over me, and still Samuel worked between my legs.

Daegan's lips nibbled at my neck and pulse before moving to my ear, his tongue stabbing inside. I felt the motion in my throbbing cunt. My mouth opened in a silent cry.

"That's it, wee one," Daegan said, his rough voice somehow gentle. "Take yer pleasure. Yer masters command it."

I crested again, and felt myself rise to the precipice a third time before Samuel settled between my legs and set himself at my opening. My eyes widened but, limp with pleasure, I couldn't move.

He pushed forward, just his head stretching me. Then he stopped and groaned.

"So tight."

Daegan lay beside me and lifted the sheet of my hair away from my neck so he could fasten his mouth there, sucking. The sensation proved too much. My body arched, straining for release and Samuel slid inside.

It felt wonderful.

Samuel pushed forward more and sagged over me, his groan louder.

"So good." He gasped. "It has been so long."

For all Samuel's care preparing me, he didn't hold back as he began to thrust. His muscles bunched as he surged into me, a steady advance and retreat that rocked my body back onto the pelts. My body accepted him, wetness pouring from my heated center.

My own muscles tightened on his thick member.

"Brenna," he breathed with reverence. One great hand splayed over my chest, sliding down to my hip. He gripped both buttocks and drove more steadily into me. The pounding brought me to the edge and tipped me over it again.

I clawed at the pelts. He lost it, driving deep to spill inside me.

"So good," he repeated. His voice back to a snarling rasp. He bent down and brushed a kiss over my lips, and Daegan took his place between my legs.

I drifted in another world as the dark haired warrior rutted fast and hard. Samuel played with my hair, brushing a finger over my lips, smearing some of my wetness over them. His finger teased my mouth open and he had me suck his finger as Daegan pounded to finish. As the dark haired warrior came with a cry, he reached down to rub my little bud. It was too much, and I tried to grab his wrist and stop him, but Samuel held my hands away.

Daegan's grin filled my vision as pleasure crashed over me again. My body shook.

I lay limp on the pelts, sweaty and spent, while the warriors congratulated themselves.

"Och, brother. I feel I am a man again," Daegan said.

"The witch spoke true." Samuel sounded very satisfied.

"Such a lovely, wee lass." Daegan threw himself down on the bed beside me. "Ye were just what we needed." He kissed me, his lips dragging from my mouth down to my neck. Settling back, he grinned over me at Samuel.

"As much as I love our scent on her, our little love needs another bath."

"But first a wee nap." Daegan sounded delighted. Neither of the warriors seemed tired at all.

Drowsy, I faded a little, my sated body growing heavy.

I realized that Daegan had kissed my scar. I pulled my damp hair over my neck to hide it, and thought back over the past minutes, trying to remember what I'd done. Had I cried out? Had ecstasy drawn an ugly noise from my throat? I'd given myself to them once again. I'd lost control.

The warriors still lay on either side of me, talking, their cocks waving in the air, slick with my juices.

Tears spilled out of my eyes.

"Oh, wee one," crooned Daegan. "It's all right." He cuddled me close, tucking my back to his front and turning so we lay on our sides, facing Samuel.

The blond stroked my hair, looking sad. ""I'm sorry, Brenna," he said. "I wish it could've been differently. We would've liked to woo you."

I blinked at him.

"It could not be." His finger traced my lip. "We were out of time."

4

When I woke from what Daegan would call a wee nap, the dark haired warrior had gone. I raised my head slowly, blinking at my surroundings. The past few...hours? Days? Had overwhelmed me and I hadn't had time to take everything in.

If I wasn't lying on a bed of furs, I'd believe it was all a dream.

The pelt-covered dais stood in the middle of the room, which was really a large cavern, hewn from rock. Along with the fireplace, iron braziers stood like sentinels around the room providing extra light and heat. Whoever designed the room found a way for air to flow freely, because the room wasn't stuffy, even with the fire.

The bed still smelled of sex, a sweet musk clinging to the furs. My body was rested but sticky, covered in the warrior's spendings.

They'd spread their slick cum over my skin as they'd told me why they'd taken me for a slave.

"We're warriors, mercenaries," Samuel explained. "We've fought for many rulers, and now that the Red King rules in peace, we've retreated here. This whole mountain is our home."

"We wanted a woman." Daegan said with a grin.

Samuel nodded. "We consulted a witch who would be right for us. She told us about you, a woman with the mark of the wolf." He traced a light finger over my face, edging close to my scar. My hair fell to cover the mark and he withdrew. "It was you, Brenna. We searched and searched, and finally tracked you. Your stepfather would take money. We tempted his greed and took you."

I tried not to look upset. They'd used a witch to find me? Why?

They'd looked for me? Searched for me? I couldn't believe it.

"So you see, Brenna, you were chosen."

No one had ever wanted me, much lest sought me out.

"We want ye, wee one," Daegan said. "We knew when we found ye, ye would be our own."

Samuel nodded. "You will learn our ways, and become ours. You will never want for anything as long as you obey us."

"It's a hard life, but it isnae so bad." Daegan stroked my breast before raising hopeful eyes to mine.

They acted like they were afraid I wouldn't accept them. But they'd given me no choice. Their happiness meant my survival.

After our talk, Samuel left and Daegan gave me more food and water, treating me like a pampered pet, before he fell asleep beside me. I'd lain awake thinking on everything they'd told me, eventually succumbing to my own exhaustion.

Now I was awake in the empty chamber. The fire burned low but it was still warm enough for to get out of bed and explore. I pulled a pelt around my shoulders, though there was no reason to be modest.

The cavern's open entrance led to a hall, and I wondered if I dare try to leave, naked and barefoot and with no idea what lay beyond the door. I walked the line of braziers, checking the walls of the chamber for cracks, escape on my mind.

I felt rather than heard someone behind me. A tingle went up my spine, a buzzing sensation that raised the hair on the back of my neck. I wasn't alone.

I whirled, but it was only Samuel rising from the pelt dais as if from slumber. I must not have noticed his large form on the dais, sleeping covered in furs.

The big warrior sat on the edge of the bed, rubbing a hand over his face.

"The wolf sleeps," he muttered. "It's been years since I've known such rest."

I stared at him.

"Come here, Brenna."

The blond leader seemed sterner than Daegan, but he'd told me not to be afraid of him. I forced myself to meet his gaze and take unflinching steps to the dais until I stood before him. If my hands gripped the pelt around my shoulders a little harder, perhaps he wouldn't notice.

The corner of his lips curled up as I stopped an arm's length away from him.

"Did you sleep well?"

I nodded.

His hand came out to touch my face, eventually tipping it to the side. I shut my eyes, willing myself not to cry. I still hated anyone examining my scars.

He covered my neck with his big hand, fingers resting over my pulse.

"It's not so bad," he said. "Just a scar. I have many."

I stared at him. It was hideous. He didn't need to tell me. He sighed.

"I wish I could talk to you."

My hand traced down the large muscles of his chest. One finger found a knotted scar.

He gave a small grin. "That was an arrow in battle. Didn't feel it at the time but collapsed afterwards. Took me three days to get back on my feet."

I stroked the marred flesh. He took his hand away from my neck, caught my hand and kissed it.

"So you see, Brenna, the scars are not marks of shame. They are marks of honor. What we survived."

I smoothed my hair over my neck, thinking on what he said.

He rose and bade me stay in the room. "It is not safe for you to venture out, little love. Do you understand?"

I nodded, and he left only to return with food. I was glad I hadn't tested this rule.

The smell of roast meat filled the room and my stomach growled. I reached for a wheaten cake and Samuel tutted.

"I wish to feed you, as Daegan did."

That had been humiliating; I blushed. My brow furrowed. Pouting, I reached for the cake again.

"Now, now, little love. Submit to my will. If you're naughty you'll be punished." He didn't sound angry, but satisfied. He settled me on his great lap and brought each morsel of food to my mouth. I ate, bite after bite often interrupted with a kiss. His lips played over mine. It wasn't unpleasant, just annoying. I was a grown woman. I could feed myself.

When he was distracted I took some food and offered it to him.

His grin stretched across his face and his muscled chest shook with a laugh. "Stubborn are we? Well that's good. We need a woman with spirit."

I fed him as he'd fed me, like a little babe. He tolerated it, even enjoyed it, if only because he thought it was funny.

When we were done I snuggled into his body, and this seemed to make him happy too. He petted and played with my hair, relaxed and in no hurry.

I was beginning to understand what they meant by me soothing them. These were warriors used to going from battle to battle. It must be nice to come home to a woman they could treat like a little pet. I supposed buying their own pleasure slave was more convenient than leaving the mountain to seek out a prostitute.

I sighed, and Samuel pushed my hair away from my face.

"What are you thinking, little love? I wish I knew."

For the first time in my life, I was glad I was mute, so I couldn't be forced to tell him.

Instead, we kissed and then his hand delved between us, finding my slippery cunny. He stroked me until my eyes glazed and my mouth fell open. Then he burrowed under the pelts to put his mouth between my legs, licking me until I felt the familiar rush of pleasure, and then rising up over me, taking me his great body rocking over mine, dominating, claiming.

I lay sated for a time and he went to get water. Idly I wondered whether it was night or day.

Samuel came back and set me in his lap again.

"You were not a virgin," he said in a matter-a-fact tone. "Did you have a lover?"

I shook my head, my hands smoothing my hair over my scars.

He frowned. "He abused you, didn't he? Your father?"

Stepfather, I silently corrected and nodded. My eyes flicked down and I turned my head so my hair fell over my face. My blond master stroked the hair back gently.

"You could not cry out."

I had fought, though. Would my sisters be able to fight as I had?

Samuel mistook my distress. "You're safe now. He will never touch you again."

His words did nothing to reassure me. Even now my stepfather would be home telling them...what? That I'd died? That men had come and taken me?

The twins were young, but the sister just younger than me, Fleur, would guess the truth: my stepfather had done away with me, one way or another. Would she be smart enough to hold her tongue, or would she speak up and be beaten? How soon would my stepfather start to prey on her and then the two younger ones?

"Hey." My blond master cupped my chin. I blinked back tears, trying to refocus on him. I could not think about my old life, I had to focus on survival, and then escape.

"You're all right now little love. I won't let anything happen to you." This last phrase came as a growl, and I hid my shiver at the reminder of the type of man who controlled my life.

"There is much for you to learn, but we will teach you. The witch chose well for us."

His hand guided my face forward, and I submitted to his kisses, even as his mouth moved down my neck, pressing against the scar. These warriors were obsessed with the mark.

To distract him, I did something daring. I ducked my

head and kissed the arrow mark on his chest. He sucked in a breath as I swirled my tongue around the raised weal.

"Oh, little love. You were made for us. We will be good to you, I swear."

As he kissed me again, Daegan strode into the room. We broke apart to watch the dark haired warrior strip off his jerkin and boots. I noticed a little silver in his black beard, matching the silver wolf pelt he wore.

"How was the hunt?" Samuel asked.

Daegan shrugged, taking a swig of water and wiping his mouth. His eyes stayed fixed on me, glowing gold.

"Go to him, Brenna." Samuel chuckled. "Give my brother a kiss."

I crawled across the pelts, smiling in greeting. The dark haired man grinned and accepted my chaste touch of lips, then cupped my head in his hands and kissed me deeply.

When he was done he rested his forehead against mine for a moment. "Thank ye, lass." His voice seemed to return to him, he and Samuel chatted about the hunt and other warriors for a few minutes, while Daegan ate some meat, offering bits to me. I accepted quietly, following my role, my ears alert for any clue for escape.

At last, Daegan reached down and tugged a lock of my hair. "Are ye enjoying yerself, Brenna?"

I hesitated, then nodded shyly.

"Ye are very beautiful."

This time the compliment didn't make me cringe. These men were warriors stuck in a mountain top camp. Of course they thought the only woman around for a hundred miles was the most beautiful thing they'd seen.

I smiled at him and raised up onto my knees, reaching for him. I set a hand on his chest, feeling his muscles flex under my palm as I kissed him. He tasted of wood and wild.

I wanted more. I slanted my head, as Samuel had done, and fed on the corner of his mouth, begging for a slip of his tongue. He rewarded me, drinking deeply.

When we were done I burned all over. I barely heard Daegan comment. "She's a quick learner."

"Aye."

"My wolf is calm," Daegan remarked, still holding me.

"As is mine."

"Better than seeking a priest to exorcise the demon," Daegan said with a sly look at Samuel. "All the praying and sacrifice, and what you needed was a sweet maiden to lie with."

Samuel growled, an unhappy sound. My body stiffened.

For a moment no one spoke. The room seemed colder.

Daegen's hands soothed up and down my back, and the edge of his mouth quirked in a little smile.

"I've upset my warrior brother." Daegan turned me to face the blond, who was staring at the stone walls, brooding. "It is your duty to make him feel better. Go to him, Brenna."

My dark haired master set me on my feet and gave me a little push. The short walk took ages. I stared at the rigid line of Samuel's shoulders.

But when I reached him and put a hand on his arm, he softened.

"Little love," he sighed, drawing me between his thick, muscled legs. "So sweet and so pure."

Even with him seated on the rock and me standing, he still was taller. I leaned in to kiss him, feeling his beard, softer than it looked, brush against my face.

His big hands came to cup my head. I waited for him to start kissing me again, sending his hands exploring so he would tease me to pleasure and ready me to rut but he seemed content to just hold me close.

Daegan moved around the cavern, feeding the braziers. "Perhaps ye can tell our wee savior the tale."

Samuel shot his warrior brother an annoyed look, but the tension drained out of him as he spoke.

"I was born in the Northern Way. Across the sea, a few days sail. I had a life and family there, but I was a warrior in service to my king."

"Tell her yer name," Daegan huffed a laugh.

"It was Sigmund, for my father's father." A ghost of a smile breached Samuel's mouth only to quickly fall away. "Then a witch came—a volva, as we Norsemen call them—who worked spells for the king. She said she would make us invincible. We all competed to be the best, worthy of the spell. When the time came, she turned us into monsters." His hand absently petted my hair.

"Great warriors," Daegan said. "Unstoppable during the killing rage."

"Aye," Samuel said softly. "But the beast eats our humanity." The blond lapsed into a brooding silence.

Daegan came close to explain the rest. "Samuel left Norway to fight for his king, and eventually put his sword up for hire. When I first met him, he professed fealty to the White Christ, and changed his name from Sigmund to Samuel." Daegan regarded his warrior brother. "You thought the Christian magic would heal you."

The blond nodded sadly. "It did not. I fasted and prayed, and the beast only grew stronger."

"We have tamed it."

Samuel lifted golden eyes to mine. "Brenna has."

"Aye."

I wrinkled my brow, looking from one to another.

"You calm the wolf," Samuel said.

I nodded. I knew this was important, even if I didn't understand.

"Little lass, you do not know how precious you are."

Then Samuel grew tired of talking, for he cupped my face and kissed it, and I leaned into the pull of his lips. His mouth possessed mine, silently promising all good things, before kissing down my neck to suck on the tender skin of my neck. My head fell back, and Daegan was there, pushing back my hair and kissing my other shoulder.

Too late I realized that his lips had traced down my scars.

It was my turn to stiffen, and them to quiet me.

"Come, lass." Daegan drew me to the cavern of springs where he bathed me thoroughly, rubbing oil into every crevice and scraping it off before bidding me rinse off.

I submitted, happy to get clean of their seed, even though I had the feeling they'd want to paint me with it again soon enough.

When he finished, Daegan handed me the oil and strigil.

"Your turn, lass." He grinned and turned his back to me. For a long time, I rubbed my hands over the broad expanse, enjoying every muscle. The great bunched muscles of his shoulder, the long lean ones alongside his spine and the small, knotted ones around his ribs.

He practically purred as I anointed him, frowning a little as I carefully scraped the oil away with the strigil. He plunged into the pool, splashing and rearing up, shaking water out of his hair.

I waited on the edge of the pool, and he beckoned me to join him, grinning when I hesitated. My hair was almost dry.

He came at me, wading with water droplets flying, a

playful look on his face. I backed up a few steps, then decided to risk it and run.

He caught me after a few steps, tossed me on his shoulder and carried me to the pool, dunking me. I came up annoyed, beginning to understand why Samuel sometimes gazed at his warrior brother with frustration. I swatted the water, sending a little spray towards him.

He grabbed me again. "Wee one, yer too courageous by half, to fight with me."

I don't know what possessed me, but I pretended to bite him.

His eyes lit and he wrestled with me, his movements light and quick and still playful. I could tell he was holding back from his full strength.

Still, when he dunked me again, I twisted and swam away, popping up and sticking out my tongue at him. Eyes bright, he chased me with a growl and for a moment I was really frightened, but when he caught me his hands were gentle.

"I got ye," he growled, my heart beat faster. "Yer mine now." He picked me up and carried me to the dry stone, laying me on a sitting rock. I lay stretched before him like a sacrifice on an altar, my chest heaving. What would he do with me?

"Lie still now, Brenna. I'm going to get my reward."

I stayed put while he went to grab a few things, but I couldn't help sitting up and cowering a little when he set two things beside me: the jar of oil, and a blade.

"Shhh, it's all right lass. Calm yerself. I'm going to shave ye."

His tone relaxed me, then his words penetrated and I scrambled up. He caught me and laid me down again

"Now, now Brenna."

"Need help brother?" Samuel entered, a loincloth draped around his giant hips. Before I knew it, the blond sat at my back, cradling me and pulling my legs apart.

"Shhh," Samuel hushed me as Daegan poured out the oil. "Be good for my warrior brother."

"I won't hurt ye, lass," Daegan told me softly. His fingers stroked my lower lips, coating them generously with oil. "Dinnae move and I won't even nick ye with the blade. You'll be all soft and smooth for us."

With a wicked smile, Daegan started sharpening the blade. I squirmed on Samuel's lap.

"Still, Brenna." The blond's voice made my body freeze. "This is what we wish. You will obey."

"Though if ye don't, it'll be a pleasure to see ye punished," Daegan added with a wink.

My eyes widened. For all their talk of caring for me, they were threatening to beat me?

Samuel sighed and explained Daegan's teasing. "Your punishment would not be harsh"

"Just a wee spanking." Daegan looked delighted at the prospect. "Though yer bum will sting because it's wet. Is that what you want, Brenna?"

I shook my head.

"Good lass. Now lie back and relax, and I'll get you all smooth for us to lick." The black haired warrior approached with the blade, and I showed my displeasure by kicking out.

"Och, careful, lass, the knife is sharp."

But I wasn't in the mood to be placated. In the past day, I'd grown more comfortable with the warriors, and forgotten too much of my fear, for as Samuel gripped me tighter, his hand came near my mouth and I bit him.

He only chuckled and clamped his hand over my mouth.

"Biting us already? Not in the throes of passion. Oh, little love you are so brave."

Before I knew it, he had flipped me over his knee and swatted my bottom once. It didn't hurt but I knew it was a warning.

"Your choice, Brenna. Submit to the shaving, or to your punishment. I can spank you as long and hard as you want."

I made my decision, thrashing and trying to fight to get off his lap. My struggles made no difference. One great leg weighed down mine, and he caught my flailing hands before smacking my bottom again. I stilled at the force, not quite strong enough to sting, but serious.

"That's one."

I struggled and he smacked the other cheek hard enough for me to catch my breath. "That's two." The sting worked through me, telling me to stop this mad experiment, and obey.

I let my body go limp over his legs in submission.

Daegan chuckled. "Seems she learned her lesson."

Anger burned through me. It seemed, in the face of their coddling and gentle treatment, I had lost all good sense.

Samuel held his hand to my face. "Kiss me to thank me for your punishment."

I contemplated this, then tried to bite him again. A stupid move, I soon realized.

"Not quite," Samuel told Daegan. "But soon." The blond's great hand beat down, covering every inch of my backside. The spanking hurt but the warrior obviously wasn't using even one iota of his full strength. It was nothing like the beating I expected, and in the end it almost felt nice for every so often the warrior stopped and rubbed my bottom. The massage muted the slight sting. After a few minutes, I felt warm and floaty, even when Samuel's swats reached a crescendo. The blows came down harder and harder, then stopped.

"Almost there?" Daegan asked.

"Aye." Samuel's fingers slid between my legs. "She's soaked." He played in my folds until I bucked my hips a little.

"Well, Brenna? Are ye ready to be good? If ye are we'll give ye a reward..."

I let myself go limp over Samuel's lap.

"Smart lass," Samuel laughed and rubbed my back and bottom. Whatever small pain I'd felt faded quickly away leaving a deep aching desire.

My face was flushed and my body relaxed when Samuel helped me up. The two warriors propped me between them and finished the job of shaving me while I submitted, desperate to cum.

"There we are. All smooth." I felt hot breath blow over my lower lips and sighed. "Now for your reward."

Daegan took his time, swirling his tongue around my newly shaved center while Samuel held me and stroked my breasts.

Despite my captive position and chastised bottom, I felt comfortable and safe. In only a few days, these warriors had molded me into the perfect object of pleasure. I marveled at how happy I was in my new role. For the first time in my life, I felt truly accepted and loved.

That sudden realization made me blink. Worry flicked through me, though it couldn't last long in my relaxed state. More dangerous than violence and beatings were bonds of kindness and love. They were holding me here, making me forget who I truly was: Brenna, scarred and sold as a slave, the only one who could stand between my sisters and my lecherous stepfather.

This thought fluttered through my head but before it could take root, Daegan shifted between my legs and I focused on him.

"Do ye like yer smooth cunny?" He lay his cheek on my thigh, his beard scratching me lightly. Wet poured from me and he inhaled, his eyes glowing brighter. He began laying kisses on my inner thighs and soft lips, waiting for me to admit my struggles had been in vain.

Setting my jaw, I reached down and tried to tug his head forward, to force him to lick me as I liked. Daegan caught my hands in surprise.

Samuel chuckled so hard, his laugh shook me as I lay back on his chest. I shot him an annoyed look.

"She grows bolder," Samuel said to Daegan in an approving tone.

"Aye, she's a courageous one. But it is a pleasure to teach her to mind." Holding my hands away, Daegan used his tongue to tame me, laving up and down my soft, wet heat until I writhed and gasped. He pulled away with a wicked smile.

"What do ye say, Brenna. Are ye glad to be shaved?"

I glared at him and he teased me some more. Finally I nodded vigorously, silently begging for release.

"Good lass," he praised me, using finger and little kisses on my pleasure bud to send me convulsing over the edge. All too soon, he was kissing and licking me again, and the coil of pleasure tightened in me again.

As he worshiped between my legs, his finger dipped and probed lightly at my bottom hole. I clenched and he shot me a mischievous look.

"One day, wee one," He said to me. "I will take you here while my brother takes your cunny, and we will claim you together." As his finger slipped in and out of my lower hole, I scrunched my features and made a face.

Daegan's laugh echoed around the chamber.

"You dinnae like the sound of that, lass?"

I squirmed away from his finger, still frowning.

"Brenna," Samuel warned, clutching me tighter.

"It's all right, brother," Daegan soothed. "Brenna, ye dinnae believe I can make it feel good?"

Before I could nod or shake my head, he dipped his head and fastened his mouth on my overstimulated nub. I tried to escape but between him and Samuel I couldn't move to escape Daegan's insistent tongue. My mouth opened in a silent gasp, and Samuel gripped my hair, turning my head to claim my mouth. I panted heavily, and Samuel drew back, nibbling on my lips instead. Between my legs, Daegan did the same, licking and sucking until I gasped into Samuel's kiss.

Over the next few minutes, I learned something about my two warriors: they thought the same. One would probe his tongue into my mouth, stabbing and possessing, while the other thrust his tongue into my cunny. My mouth fell open, lax, and my eyes were half lidded as two men fed on my sweet lips, one above, one below. Eventually Samuel transferred his snuffling kisses to my ears, while Daegan remained at the center of my legs, sucking on my pleasure spot until I shuddered onto the pelts.

In the languid aftermath of my release, I realized Daegan had ventured further, sweeping his tongue up between my buttocks. It felt good, but I fought to close my legs and keep him out. With a small growl, he pinned my thighs and, gripping my bum cheeks to hold them open, vigorously tongued my dark hole.

I didn't want it to feel good, but it did. I reminded myself that he'd washed me thoroughly. All the same, I was glad when he added two fingers to my cunny, stroking my sensitive pearl to another shattering climax.

"Is she ready for a good hard fucking?" Daegan asked Samuel as I lay convulsing on the pelts.

"She was born for it," Samuel growled and swung into place over me. He kissed and rubbed his bearded face against my breasts for a minute or two, letting me come down from the precipice before he spread my legs set himself at my slick center and slid inside me. The shock waves began all over again. I thrashed on his pillaging cock. His manhood stretched me but my soaking cunt accepted him.

He fucked me hard and I accepted it like I'd been made to bounce on the end of his huge rod. I lifted my legs and hitched them around his hips so he could drive deep, cursing as he came.

Without further ado, Samuel pulled out, his slickened spear still hard and jutting from his hips, and Daegan took his place. The black haired warrior drove home in a great lurching thrust that had my head flying back. He bottomed out and retreated only to do it again.

The orgasm came from deep inside me, almost breaking me. I gasped and panted and clawed at the pelts.

"Do ye see how it will be, lass? Two men unable to sate themselves on your body. We will pound yer heat and then flip you over for a good arse fucking while one takes yer sweet mouth. Then a nice long rest and a bath before we do it again."

He pulled out and rolled me over belly on the pelts. "Oil, brother. She'll take her pleasure with something in her ass."

Daegan slid back inside my wet heat but added a finger to my bottom hole, swirling and working one thick digit inside me. My body cramped around the oiled intruder. I felt full to breaking.

Samuel came to my front and set his cock at my mouth.

"Lick me," he growled, taking my hair and guiding me to clean his member.

They played with me like that for a while, Samuel using my tongue to lick him back to hardness while Daegan squeezed and rubbed my bum, finger fucking my dark entrance while his cocked remained sheathed inside my cunt.

Finally Daegan tired of playing with my ass. Samuel drew back, stroking himself off in front of my face while his warrior brother slammed hard into me. They both finished within seconds of one another, Daegan gripping my hips hard enough to leave marks, while Samuel painted my face with seed.

They spent some time spreading it over my skin, claiming me, before washing me off and carrying me to bed.

5

Time passed, and I knew not how long I stayed in the cave. It was more than a sennight, for my monthly bleeding came and went. The warriors doted on me during that time as they always did, bringing me food and taking me to bathe.

The pampering continued after my menses ended. I grew to enjoy the way they coddled and cared for me, though I wished I could communicate with them. Sometimes they lounged and spoke of their past, warrior exploits. They seemed to have battled enough for three lifetimes. At times they mentioned kings with foreign names, or kings who I had heard of, but who had died long ago.

If I could, I'd ask them about their past, and how they came to live on a mountain as a berserker clan. At times they returned from the hunt, smelling of blood, eyes bright with that strange golden light. Something in their manner sent a prickle up my spine, like they were predators and I was prey. They'd eat and bathe and sleep, speaking broken phrases in harsh, guttural tones.

But mostly they fucked me.

Their hands and long, tickling hair wrought their desire on my skin, until I was trembling and ready. Then one would mount me or another.

I did not know it was morning or evening when I woke, cocooned between two large, warm bodies. Their long hair streamed over my body, mingling with mine. Holding my breath, I listened, but they were not awake. Usually they woke me, excited hands caressing me, positioning me, mouths finding my sensitive places until I panted, ready for them. Then they took turns rutting hard and fast between my legs.

They kept me naked and most of the time they also wore no clothes beyond a leather loincloth. They seemed always hard and ready for me.

I moved a little, and felt one hard length grow against my leg.

I felt the heat roll over me, claiming me, and for the first time in a moon, I was ready before they were.

Staring at Samuel's beautiful sleeping face, my fingers sought his member and stroked it with the barest of movements. The shaft grew longer against me, I would not have thought it possible.

Behind me Daegan sighed and I reached behind me, seeking his thickness with a tentative finger.

My small hands encircled them, taking liberties.

Another sigh behind me, and echoed by Samuel, and I looked up to see a little smile playing on the blonder man's face.

"Someone's awake," he said. He opened his eyes and I blinked at the bright gold light.

"You think she's ready for us?" Daegan breathed at my ear, and I heard his smile.

"Always." Samuel came to hands and knees and rolled

me under him.

When it was over, our bodies lay twined together on the pelts.

"To think how long we went without this," Samuel said. His fingers traced my cheek. As time went on they'd stopped touching my scar, but I no longer minded as much. It had been so long since I'd left the mountain, the rest of my life seemed almost a dream.

While Daegan rose and fed the braziers, Samuel continued to stroke my face and hair. His gaze held a touch of melancholy. "So young and lovely. The beauty of a flower, meant to fade."

My brow furrowed.

"It does no good to think on this, brother," Daegan called.

"My brother has never taken a woman into his home, or his heart," Samuel looked at me, but I could feel his annoyance at Daegan's comment. "He came to be a Berserker a different way, and has never known any other life."

"I am still witch born," Daegan protested. "Unnatural."

"A monster," Samuel agreed. "Like me."

I didn't like this line of talk. Both my warriors seemed so sad, and, trapped here in the two rooms, they'd become my world. They did not seem monsters to me. Large and brutal, but also gentle and kind. At least, to me.

I thought back over all the stories they told. Some of them I assumed were tales of great heroes of old. But I had heard of Harald Fairhair, the king who united the Northern Way. He was of old, many kings before our own Red King. How could Samuel, once Sigmund have fought for a ruler who'd died so many centuries before? It didn't make sense to me. How old were they? I couldn't ask, but I searched for clues.

"Is it easier, little love, to be born a monster, or changed to one?"

"Ye chose the witch's curse," Daegan said.

"I wouldn't if I knew the truth. I lived as something other than a monster. I had a family. You never did."

"I have longed for one," Daegan said, and I could tell he was irritated.

"My wolf brother doesn't understand what I lost," Samuel told me, and Daegan let a little growl, prowling around the perimeter of the room.

I glanced back at the dark haired warrior, nervous.

Immediately Samuel looked contrite. "Calm, little love. We will not hurt you."

"It is an old quarrel," Daegan blew out a frustrated breath.

I still felt unsettled, and I didn't like it. I put my hand on Samuel's shoulder and squeezed. He captured my hand and kissed it. I reached out my other for Daegan and he came closer.

"Our little love doesn't like seeing us fight," Samuel remarked, but he didn't sound upset. He held my hand in his own massive paws, rubbing and massaging, cradling carefully like it was a fragile bird.

"She knows the way to soothe us. Come, Brenna," Daegan tugged my hand. "Let us teach you something new." He lay a pelt before the dais and helped me kneel before Samuel.

"Whenever I anger my brother it'll be up to you to settle him."

With a small smile, Samuel shifted his loincloth and drew himself out.

"Touch him," Daegan said into my ear. The dark haired

warrior crouched behind me, coaching me as I took Samuel's shaft in my hand and stroked him.

"Now yer mouth, wee one," he instructed.

As my lips brushed his cock, Samuel closed his eyes. I took it as a good sign.

The truth was I liked finding ways to please them. On my knees before the great warrior, I felt content.

My tongue touched his thick flesh and his cock jumped. I circled around the pink crown, then, at Daegan's insistence, pushed my head forward to swallow more. Samuel was too thick for me to take down very far, but I tried my best, backing off and working my mouth down again.

Daegan's fingers sifted in my hair and he worked my head up and down in a rhythm until Samuel stiffened and came. Cum spilled from my mouth and down my chest.

Samuel sat up and fed it to me, smearing it over my lips and breasts before kissing me.

"You smell of my seed," he growled happily. His golden eyes glowed.

"My turn." Daegan took a handful of my hair and tugged gently to turn me to him. I rose up on tall knees and gave him the same service. With his dark hair and golden eyes, he looked like a wicked beast, feral. For all his gentle coaxing when I serviced his brother, Daegan was more forceful with me, gripping my head and moving it up and down the shaft. I gripped his thighs and breathed through my nose until he spent himself.

Samuel tugged me to my feet. He sat on the rock, his manhood sticking straight up. I thought he wanted me to lick him again, but he took my hips and lifted me onto his cock. We both sighed as I sank down his shaft. As always, his thickness stretched me to pleasure's breaking point. His hand slipped between us and his thumb caught my pleasure nub, stroking until shockwaves radiated through me. I convulsed, my hands tearing at his hair. His mouth found my neck, licking and sucking the tender skin. His lips drifted to the thick scar tissue. I tolerated it for a few moments, before tugging his head away. A growl rumbled through his chest, but he moved on to my chest until I arched back, offering my breasts to him as he licked, teased and sucked the tender mounds.

Daegan came to prop me up and I leaned back against him, smiling as his head came down to claim my mouth. His warrior brother finished worshiping my breasts and pulled me against him. Samuel gripped my hips hard and lifted me up and down on his shaft.

Pleasure claimed me again, vibrations starting deep, deep inside me and spreading outwards through my whole body. I gasped and clawed at Samuel's arms and muscled shoulders. The big warrior roared and lay back, pulling me over him.

"Ride me," he ordered, his eyes piercing mine.

I struggled to get my limbs together.

I felt Daegan's hand smooth down my back, squeezing one butt cheek and then the other before smacking it. "Up and down, Brenna, there's a good lass. Give my brother relief."

Finding purchase on the rock, I straddled the big warrior and pushed myself up and down. My skin grew slick with sweat.

Daegan spanked me for a while to encourage me, then his fingers slipped in the crevice between my buttocks. I jerked up to escape the probing digit, and the dark haired warrior smacked my bottom again.

Samuel's fingers tugged my nipples, drawing my attention. "Faster," he grunted, and I obeyed, rocking over him as he pulled my nipples to control the pace. The pain made me clench down on the blond's giant cock, and he grabbed my hips and pounded me from beneath until he came with a roar.

I'd barely recovered before Daegan gripped my hair and pulled me off Samuel's cock.

"Lick him clean," the dark-haired warrior ordered hoarsely, "While I take ye from behind."

Bent over Samuel's prone body, I obeyed. In the heat of arousal, Daegan's usual joking manner disappeared, but I didn't mind. They'd primed my body for fucking, and I reveled in the feel of the dark haired warrior's hard thrusts while I worshiped Samuel's turgid member.

Daegan pulled out before climaxing and painted my back with his seed. I'd grown used to our coupling ending with me covered in their cum, but this time I was well and truly covered. The warriors seemed so pleased, I was afraid they would not let me bathe.

At last Daegan led me to the heated springs. He left me while I splashed and bathed. I enjoyed getting clean, both using the oil and strigil and rinsing the oil off. I stood in the shallows stroking my skin and admiring my full breasts, narrow waist flaring into wide hips and a rounded bottom. My body felt full of desire and sated at the same time. I almost hummed with the thought of returning to the dais and taking the two warriors again.

Floating in the water, I closed my eyes and let my hands idly play over my body.

A thought struck me and I surged to my feet, languid mood gone. I was in heat. Again.

I covered my face with my hands.

Surely it could not be. A month had passed and I was still here. I had forgotten myself. I had forgotten my sisters helpless to my stepfather's lechery. The warriors had chained me with bonds of care and kindness. They'd treated me so well, I'd forgotten my duty.

I'd even forgotten my hideous face.

The water rippled around my body, marring my reflection, mocking me. I had but to look and I could remember it all.

But it was too late--my womb cramped for my warrior lovers to take me. Even my body was my enemy.

My mouth opened in soundless scream.

I staggered back to the room and pulled a pelt around me. I had no boots or clothes, but I could not delay. For the first time since they'd brought me to the cavern, I entered the hall and moved towards the cold outside air, escape on my mind. Samuel had told me never to venture out by myself and the threat of danger had been enough to keep me. That and their caressing touches, so welcome after a lifetime of being an outcast. In the soft light of love, I was blind to my true ugly self. The witch had indeed chosen well.

Awash in bitter thoughts, I stepped out of the cave and onto the mountain ledge, blinking in the light. The sun hung low in the sky—evening or morning I did not know.

A path led from the lip of the cave down the mountain, and for a second it seemed I could escape.

Movement caught my eye and I startled as the shapes emerged from shadow, the mottled fur a natural camouflage against the stone.

Everywhere I looked, I saw wolves.

Just like that, my dream of escape turned into a nightmare.

I backed away from the path off the mountain, one hand clutching the pelt, the other covering my scar. Pitiful protection from these beasts who now surrounded me, a few even cutting off my re-entrance into the cave. I was trapped on a mountain with a pack of wolves, my earliest tormentors.

My mouth opened and worked in a cry no one could hear.

A wolf had taken my voice, and changed my life forever. And now wolves would take my life.

There was one way open to me: the edge of the cliff. Tears now streaming down my face, I inched backwards.

A dark wolf darted out before the rest. He didn't growl, just stood, alert, watching me.

That's when I realized all the wolves had golden eyes.

My head started weaving back and forth. No, it could not be.

A golden wolf, larger than all the rest, ran out from the pack and drew abreast with the dark one, and I knew then beyond all doubt, here was Samuel and Daegan. The berserkers were not men given to rage like beasts. They were beasts. Wolves.

Mouth still stretched in a scream, I turned and ran. My feet pounded on the stone. I could not escape them, but the ledge ended a few feet from me. I could throw myself over and die.

A great blast behind me drove me to the ground. My hair blew as if tossed by the wind, but the air was still.

"No," a snuffling growl came from behind me. "Brenna!"

I scrambled to my feet and whirled. The dark wolf only a foot away, its mouth open and tongue panting. Was there sorrow in its golden eyes?

I put my hands up in a gesture for it to stay away. Samuel crouched a few feet behind the wolf, bent over on hands and knees. He was naked but for a loincloth, as I had seen him many times. "Brenna," he choked out, and then repeated in a clearer human voice, "Please."

In my haste to escape, I misjudge how close I was to the edge. One tiny step backwards and I started falling. The wolf leapt.

Jaws snapped onto the pelt and jerked me forward. I clung to the fur robe as the wolf dragged me back onto the mountain ledge. For a second my feet kicked over the rock, in the empty air, but the thick pelt saved me. That, and the crushing jaws of a wolf.

Samuel leaned over me, worry scribed in every line of his face.

"Brenna." His hands roved over my body, checking me. Beside the blond warrior, the dark wolf whined.

Samuel lifted and carried me to the room with the pelts. I stared into the golden eyes, piecing it all together. These were the berserkers of old. Over the centuries, they'd fought for kings and different countries, finally settling in the highlands, secluded and alone where no one would know they were wolves. They needed a slave to sate their lusts, and consulted a witch, who told them to find me. For who would miss such a hideous peasant woman, whose flesh already bore the scars of their kind.

I lay on the pelt, pain bubbling through me despite Samuel's gentle ministrations. He stripped my dress away and wrapped my throat, then lay beside me stroking my hair from my face and speaking to me in a soothing tone. "Brenna, I am sorry. I wish I could've told you another way. I'd do anything to take away your fear."

His hand brushed my scar and I stiffened. Closing my eyes, I turned my back on him. Samuel settled one great arm around me, pulling me back to his front. His sigh blew through my hair.

"Please, little love. Do not fear us. I do not know what gave you those scars. A wolf or a normal dog, or one such as ourselves. We are witch born. The beast lives inside us, and it can be sated. Somehow you..." He paused to tip his head into my hair and take a deep breath, as the warrior did so often. "...you soothe the wolf."

I scrunched my face, willing myself not to cry. It wasn't fair. To have my destiny changed, twice, both times by beasts. It did not matter that I loved my warrior masters. A lifetime of suffering was enough to wipe the tender moments away.

A snuffling sound caught my attention. The dark wolf stood beside the dais, shaking its head this way and that as if it wore an invisible coat it wanted to claw off. I stiffened and started to scramble away, but Samuel held me, facing the wolf.

"That is Daegan. He is trying to change back into a man for you, so he can comfort you."

The beast stopped and whined, a desperate, pathetic sound, even to my frightened ears.

"I called on pack magic to change quickly, so I might speak to you," Samuel explained. "Each wolf gave me aid and it will be awhile before they recover. But Daegan is strong. His power is almost equal to mine. Even weakened, he may be able shift."

The wolf ducked its head again, and whined. Massive as it was, it did not seem as frightening as before.

"Look at him, Brenna. He suffers, because you are afraid of him. You returned our humanity to us. Please do not hate us, and take it away."

Samuel and I watched the black beast struggle for a long while. Its body shook as if worried by a thousand tormenting bees. A part of me wanted to comfort it.

The blond warrior spoke again. "For years we have fed the beast with violence. Centuries of fighting and death. The killing rage is sweet, when it is upon us. But it leached us of all goodness, until we were hollow inside." He rolled me to face him, but I still heard the wolf snuffling and fighting to shift behind me. "I did everything to cling to humanity. Sought out women, carried out good deeds. Even renounced the warrior way, took a vow of piety and changed my name to become a priest. But my prayers were not answered."

His great hand covered my scars and for once I didn't flinch away, held in thrall by his story and his eyes. "I became a scholar, and sought a witch. She told us to look for one who'd been marked by a wolf. Daegan passed through your village, saw you bathing in the stream, and knew." His head bent again, pressing into the curve between my neck and shoulder. "Please, little love. Do not leave us for the darkness. We need you."

I stared at the dark wolf, then touched my scars another wolf had made.

When I was a child a wolf marred me. Today one wolf saved me, but the wolves had saved me long before then. One moon ago.

They thought themselves monsters, these berserker wolves, but I knew worse monsters. My stepfather was one of them.

Samuel shifted his head from my shoulder and I rose and went to where Daegan lay, exhausted in a failed attempt to change. His ears pricked up but he didn't move. Large as he was, he seemed as tame as a pet dog.

A few feet away, I knelt and stretched out my hand. My whole body shook with fear, but I embraced the terror. I accepted the wolf; it would accept me or I would die.

The berserker Daegan raised his head.

I felt the loops of power, the pack magic that Samuel described. I did not know how I felt it, but I did. The warmth spread through me, carrying me forward to my dark haired wolf.

Outside, one by one, the wolves began to howl. An aching melody echoed down the hall. A sad, yet triumphant sound. No wolf was angry, or slavering for my flesh. I felt buoyed by the impromptu chorus, lifted up.

With fluid predator strength, Daegan rose and padded to my side.

I hugged the wolf, burying my face in its dark fur, smelling the scent of woods and wild. I felt Samuel at my back and the first tingles of power before the blond tugged me away. In a brief blast of golden light and magic, Daegan shifted.

Then I embraced the man.

6

I slept between the two men as always. After the change, Daegan struggled to speak, his golden eyes communicating his longing. A few snuffling attempts at speech and I lay my finger against his mouth. I didn't need words of comfort. Taking both warrior's hands, I led them to the bed. We curled up together. Daegan was the first to fall asleep, and all the days of him returning from the hunt, smelling of blood and wanting to only eat, sleep or rut made sense.

"So now, Brenna, do you understand?" Samuel asked. I nodded.

When the beast took over, it took their human speech and the effects took some time to shake off. Samuel and Daegan were leaders of the pack, Samuel at the head and Daegan a close second. After centuries of fighting, the beast dominated their human side. They needed a panacea, someone or thing that could bring their beast back under control.

They searched and consulted a witch, and then found me.

I didn't know why I could calm the wolf, but it didn't matter. I had saved them.

"You know who we are and you accept us," Samuel told me. "We need you here with us for all time, Brenna, though sometimes I wish there was another way. I know what it is like to have a witch speak and change your life."

I slept a little, and when I woke the two berserkers were watching me.

Samuel set a silver torc at my hand, an ornament of old. Warriors sometimes wore arm rings in fealty to their chief or king. This looked like both the jewelry of a princess and the collar of a slave. Perhaps it was both, something in between. A band to honor a savior and mark a thrall.

I touched it.

"We wish ye to accept it," Daegan said. His voice was still husky and his eyes glowed, but he was fully man.

"This will mark you as ours among the wolves."

I stared at the torc. They were asking me to make a decision, not to stay or go, but to accept my place. I was ready to accept, but for one thing.

It took some time making hand gestures, but I made them understand.

"You worry for your family," Samuel interpreted.

I gestured to my hair and curvy body then stretched my hand out indicating a shorter height.

"Yer sisters," Daegan guessed.

"You want to know they are cared for?"

I hesitated, not knowing how to tell them that I feared my stepfather might be a threat.

Large fingers tipped my head to face Samuel's. The big blond stared into my eyes. I felt a tingling down my spine, but held still.

After a long moment, Samuel blew out a sigh. "You do not trust your mother's husband around them."

I nodded vigorously while Daegan and Samuel exchanged glances.

"Brenna," Daegan called. "Do ye want us to take care of the threat?" The usually playful dark-haired warrior looked very serious.

I nodded.

"And if we do, you will stay and live among us? Willingly?"

I nodded and reached for the torc, setting it into my lap and staring into one pair of golden eyes, then another.

I'd made my choice. It was up to them.

"Back in a day," Daegan said. He kissed me and left.

I tucked my legs to my chest and wrapped my arms around them.

Samuel prowled around me, restless. Every so often he lifted his head, scenting the air. I knew he could smell my heat.

We waited.

Shadows crawled in the corners. I must have eaten and slept, for the next thing I knew, the smell of blood filled the chamber.

"Brenna," Samuel called.

I rose, pulling a pelt around me instead of a dress. I was a berserker's mate now. I could walk among the wolves naked; my lovers would protect me.

Together the blond leader and I walked down the hall to the ledge outside the cave, where a pack of giant weres waited. Daegan stepped forward in man form, hunched a little and moving with predator silence. The air prickled with the smell of blood. I approached him and he held up a basket dripping red.

I knew before I looked what I would find inside.

"Daegan tells me the kill stank of perversion. When your sister found the body, she laughed."

I set the basket containing my stepfather's head on the ground. My sisters Sabine, Muriel, and Fleur were safe now.

Daegan and Samuel followed me back to the chamber. I pointed to the bathing cave, wrinkling my nose, and the dark haired warrior disappeared to bathe.

When Daegan returned, naked and dripping wet, Daegan found me sitting on the dais with the torc in my lap.

Raising my chin, I handed it to Samuel.

Daegan held up my hair while Samuel bent the torc as if it were made of straw and closed it around my neck. I touched the cool metal and felt a strange hum of power, as if the torc was an object of magic. The silver both covered some of my scar, and drew attention to it.

Rising on tiptoe, I drew Samuel's head down and kissed him, then Daegan, before leading them back to the dais.

We claimed one another while the wolves howled outside.

∽

ONE MOON LATER, I stood on the edge of the great market, watching my mother set up her stall. My twin sisters played in the grass while Fleur worked beside my mother.

"We found a merchant who will pay good price for their wares," Samuel had told me. "And every month the eldest sister finds fresh meat on their doorstep. We will watch over them."

As I watched, I felt a flare of power behind me in the forest, signaling a wolf changing into man form. My sister Fleur's head jerked sharply in our direction, and she started to move towards my hiding place. I stepped back, but my mother called Fleur, and my sister went to help her, still frowning in puzzled thought.

I turned my back on my family and headed deeper into the forest, where two men waited for me in the thick underbrush. One dark, one blond, huge forms hunched and lurking in the shadows lit with two pairs of golden eyes.

∼

DAEGAN, Samuel and Brenna's story continues in Mated to the Berserkers. Read on for an excerpt.

MATED TO THE BERSERKERS - EXCERPT

The buck stood grazing on the edge of the forest stream, its crown of proud antlers reflected in the rippling water. I watched hidden in the shadows. I'd tracked the buck for miles, loosening my muscles and enjoying the hunt, and I could almost taste my prey. A real wolf wouldn't be able to take down so large a quarry without its pack. A man could kill a buck with bow and arrow, and struggle to carry it back to his home. But I was neither human nor true wolf.

The wind shifted, and brought a flurry of scents. Among the usual bouquet, I smelled something sour. Another wolf, but not a familiar one. I knew the scents of my pack. This was an intruder.

The wind shifted and the buck grazed closer to my hiding place. My wolf forgot the worrying scent and focused on the prey immediately across the stream.

I Changed. In one instant the water below me reflected a man, with hard muscles and dark hair. Then an unnatural wind stirred the leaves, and in place of a man stood a great black wolf.

The buck raised its head at the unfamiliar wave of magic. It caught scent of the wolf I had become, and ran.

It was a short chase.

Afterward, licking the blood off my paw, I felt reluctant to change back. Men were slow and stupid, and bound by rules. They couldn't even smell the kaleidoscope of colors that the forest was, choosing instead to destroy everything with fire and live in smelly shacks in the mud.

Was not the world so much more beautiful as a wolf?

But beneath the simple, animal consciousness, lurked a darker beast. Even now, with the taste of blood in my mouth, the rage-filled creature struggled for dominance. I wrestled with it, shaking my wolf head as if worried by flies. My frantic inner fight brought me to the stream where I watched my canine features grow and Change into something grotesque...

My canine nose caught a pale scent, wafting all the way down from the mountain my pack called home. The smell told me a woman lived there. Not just any woman. Our woman.

Our mate.

The beast receded. Sanity returned.

I savored the woman's scent--light and cool, perfumed and perfect amid the sweaty stench of the warriors. She was waiting.

One more breath of her luscious scent, and I shifted. Paws became hands, fur became hair, and the bloodlust of the beast died as if it had never been.

I ran all the way home, carrying the buck.

At the top of the mountain path, a giant warrior stood guard, honing his axe. Wulfgar had been a deadly warrior even before becoming a Berserker. His blunt features brightened at the sight of fresh meat.

I slung the deer at his feet.

"Good hunt?" The massive warrior gave an appreciative sniff.

I grunted. After being a wolf, speech took its time returning.

Wulfgar barked an order to another wolf. "Roast the choicest bits over the fire for the Alpha's woman. Give the rest to the pack."

I nodded my thanks to Wulfgar, and the small red-headed wolf that came to collect the carcass.

"Beta," they both acknowledged me with a dip of their heads, taking care to avert their eyes from mine out of respect for my rank. Even though Wulgar stood a full head taller than me, I was slightly more dominant, if only because of my bond with the Alpha, Samuel.

A breeze swept along the face of the mountain, stirring the smoke of the fire and bringing the sweet aroma of a woman to me.

I left the fire and entered the cave, following the stone passageway to the quarters I shared with Samuel...and her.

As I walked down the hall, the sweet scent grew stronger. I paused in the doorway to our rooms. Inside Samuel lounged in wolf form, tawny streaks in his grey hide.

I nodded to him and headed straight for the pelt covered dais we used as a bed, to peek at the dark-haired woman burrowed in the furs.

Still asleep, Samuel spoke through our bond.

Best we stop wearing her out, I grinned at him.

He almost smiled. He'd been a Berserker so long, and spent almost a century half mad with magic. I'd been the tether holding him to the world, keeping him from a killing rage that would rape his mind. We'd fought Samuel's beast, together, and searched high and low for the woman the witch told us would save him—a woman marked by the wolf.

Brenna.

A deep breath, and the scent of her filled my lungs. The wolf quieted. I hadn't even realized how restless it was until I saw her, and relaxed. She smelled of moss and pine and the soft secret places in the forest that are safe.

No wonder our great Alpha basked at her feet in wolf form, his tongue lolling out like a puppy. After centuries of fighting, we'd finally found home.

I started to lie beside her on the dais and Samuel gave a half growl.

I won't wake her, I said through the bond. *Not just yet. I just want to lie close to her.*

I waited for his nod, then stretched out, tucking myself around her in the pelts.

Edging closer, I buried my face in her wealth of dark hair.

She stirred.

I bowed my body around her, letting her warmth seep into me, reveling in the soft curves of her body.

Beside the dais, Samuel watched in wolf form, panting happily.

My hand slipped between the pelts to cup her breast. I played with the soft handful, feeling her nipple harden and body come alive. I longed to hear her soft sigh of arousal, and a few seconds later, I was rewarded with the lovely sound.

We kept our beloved naked most of the time, furnishing her with a few dresses and wraps but mostly keeping the brazier burning around the room. Samuel and I lived in wary alert to protect our woman from any other. Even our pack, our warrior brothers, weren't to be trusted. Her scent was a siren call, too compelling and sweet. We kept her safe in this chamber, hidden from the world.

I closed my eyes and inhaled, giving the wolf what it craved, filling my lungs with the essence of her.

My body throbbed with need.

"Brenna," I breathed onto the back of her neck.

She sighed and everything in me focused on that slight sound. Her head tilted and her hair spilled off her neck, revealing the spidery scars at her throat, the scar evidence of a brutal wound she sustained as a child. The attack took her voice. It was a wonder it didn't take her life, but she survived.

Now she was ours.

Brenna shifted against me and my body responded, leaping to life, blood rushed to my groin. I grunted a little as I slipped an arm under her and tightened my hold on her, drawing her against my chest.

She wasn't a small woman by human standards, but compared to us, she was slight and perfect. Her softness made her all the more inviting.

Her bottom brushed my cock and I groaned into her hair.

Daegan, Samuel chided via the bond. *You woke her.*

"Couldnae be helped," I said out loud. "Such a bonny temptation."

My hand started exploring the softness of her breast, the smooth dip of her belly ending in the gently flaring hips.

"Wake up lass," I crooned in her ear as my fingers played south of her belly. "I'll make it worth yer while."

Her eyes fluttered open.

Not for the first time, I wished that our beloved could speak. The scars on her throat made her mute. Though she never had any trouble making her feelings known, I would give anything to hear her say my name.

My fingers searched for that wet sweet place between her legs, working to draw out a gasp. I smiled when I heard it leave her lips.

She sighed again and I wondered how awake she was. Then she shook her bottom against my groin. Her cheek curved with a smile and I knew she was awake.

"Naughty lass," I said, "getting me all worked up for ye." I propped myself on an elbow above her. "Don't ye know you're already enough of a temptation?"

She lay on her back, blinking up at me with those sultry, sleepy eyes.

I couldn't take it any longer; I leaned down and claimed her mouth. My fingers dipped and swirled between her legs, making her hips dance.

Magic pulsed through the room as Samuel made the Change from wolf to man. He took his place close to us.

Shifting over Brenna, I kissed my way down the slopes of her neck and breasts, not stopping until I tasted the secret place between her legs.

She tensed but I held her legs open, lapping at the pink center while she writhed.

At her head, Samuel captured our beloved's mouth, his hand at her breast. With fingers, lips and tongues, we worked our beloved's body until she vibrated between us like a lute's string, strummed to the point of breaking. Samuel let her mouth go and nibbled at her ear while I nibbled below. From her wild gasps and writhing, her body teetered on the edge of pleasure. We pinned her between us until she crested and shattered.

As she panted to catch her breath, Samuel and I shared a grin.

"Beautiful," he said so Brenna could hear.

"Aye." I nuzzled her inner thigh.

After a minute she blinked, raising her head. Without speaking, Samuel and I switched places. He pulled her to hands and knees and positioned himself behind her. She moved obediently as he propped her hips high and reached down to tease her folds.

I guided my beloved's head to my aching cock. She obeyed my silent command, sucking me so deeply my knees almost gave out.

"Och, lass." My hand stroked her cheek.

Samuel gripped her hips and I held Brenna's face still, preparing for his thrust. She gasped as he surged forward. The force of his movement drove her forward onto my own cock, and for a second I popped into her throat. The pressure took my breath away.

The bond between the Alpha and I hummed in harmony as we sawed our beloved's body between us. I cradled her face carefully as she rocked back and forth between us.

Samuel reached under again and stimulated her to another orgasm. Her gasps leaked around my cock and I came cursing, my hand fisted in her dark hair.

Pleasure poured down the bond between us, and Samuel's eyes glazed with lust. His canines flashed as he teetered on the brink between man and mindless beast.

I pulled out of my beloved's mouth with a pop, backing away at Samuel's signal. The giant blond warrior knelt naked behind our woman, his golden hair hanging about his shoulders. He smoothed a hand down Brenna's back, steadying her, readying her for a good fucking.

With a growl, he surged forward. His hips beat into her backside and a slapping sound filled the cavern. As Samuel kept up the brutal pace, Brenna's hands fisted into the pelts, her breath hitching in her broken throat.

"Cum." With the order, Samuel's palm smacked down on the side of her upturned ass. Brenna's eyes rolled back into her head as she obeyed, thrashing.

Samuel shuddered over her, large hands holding her hips up as he finished deep inside her. Once he pulled out, he took a handful of her hair and drew her to his cock, biding her clean it with her mouth. As I watched her lick submissively, my cock hardened again. The beast within craved dominance over our beloved, demanded her sweet submission. And it did not want to stop there...

I shut off that line of thought and flopped onto my side beside her, toying with her hanging breasts and admiring the flushed state of her skin.

"Lovely, lovely lass," I told her, and murmured the words I wished were true. "Ye were meant for us."

∼

MUCH LATER I stood guard over our beloved while Samuel was gone. I watched her sleep, noting the fall of raven dark hair, the cheeks pale as moonlight.

Mine, said the wolf, and I wanted to agree. She was ours in every way we could make her. We'd bought her from her family a few moons ago, and kept her in our lair, away from the pack. She seemed to accept us. We brought her news of her remaining family--her three sisters thrived in the village. Two moons ago her mother died, we brought her the news. Samuel asked if she wanted to see the grave and Brenna shook her head no.

She'd left her old life, for us. And every time we claimed her, we felt we'd come home. But did she truly belong here?

She is ours. Samuel felt my uncertainty and spoke through the bond.

For as long as we keep her. I reminded him.

Why would we ever let her go?

I sent him the memory of hunting the buck earlier. *It happened again. I almost lost control of the beast.*

Silence. Samuel did not want to acknowledge that what we feared most might happen--the very beast Brenna soothed might rage again.

The Berserker rage was legendary on the battlefield. Many kings used it to gain power. In times of peace, the beast craved bloodshed. The magic that made us wolves carried a taint, and would drive us to madness. That was the price of our great power.

Brenna didn't know any of this. She didn't know several of the pack had succumbed to the beast and met their fate. When the beast took their mind, Samuel was waiting. More than a few had died, necks snapped and bodies flung off the mountain by the raging Alpha. Not because his control broke; because theirs did. Samuel protected the pack, even from its own members. But there was only so much he could do to keep the taint from spreading. We were warriors seasoned with many battles, but could not win the war for our minds. Before we'd consulted the witch to find Brenna, we were losing.

I remembered the nights when the beast howled for blood...

Tell me what happened, Samuel said finally. *How did you regain control?*

I caught our beloved's scent.

Just as the runes foretold. She soothes the beast.

I reached out and ran a finger over our beloved's smooth cheek. Her skin was so soft, so sweetly scented. Tonight she smelled like moonlight on the snow, and secrets kept deep in the earth...things no man had words for, things that only a wolf would understand.

My hand closed around her neck. Her pulse beat against my palm.

Both Samuel and I feared the day she'd wake and discover who we truly were. Not just werewolves, but Berserkers, cursed with tainted magic. We told Brenna not to fear the wolf, but never mentioned what she truly should fear: the beast.

She'd seen us in wolf form, but she hadn't seen the beast. Not even close.

Did she know when we took her, hard and fast, without thought, what monster lurked in our minds? Did she sense how much the beast wanted to hurt her?

My fingers closed over her throat. Once I had almost lost control. It could never happen again.

We cannot keep hiding the beast from her, Samuel's thought echoed across the bond. I snatched my hand away guiltily. *She will meet it, one way or another.*

Nay, it's too dangerous. This was why we'd spent centuries alone.

If she is to be our mate, she needs to meet the pack, learn our ways. We can't keep her inside forever.

But, I struggled to put my feelings into words. *What if she meets the beast, and can no longer love us?*

Can she truly love us, if she doesn't know what we are?

The beast does not love. It will try to destroy her.

I held my breath until Samuel answered, *Pray that it does not succeed.*

MATED TO THE BERSERKERS

A Highlander and Viking claim their woman...
For over a hundred years, the Berserker warriors have fought and killed for kings. There is but one enemy we cannot defeat: the beast within.

A witch told us of the one who can save us--a woman marked by the wolf. We found and claimed her. But will she accept us as mates? Can she soothe our feral nature before it is too late?

Highland werewolf Daegan never expected to defeat the curse of his bloodline. But when a prophecy tells of a woman who might cure his Berserker rage, he and his Viking warrior brother will stop at nothing to claim her.

They bring her to their mountain home and train her according to pack rules. She is their captive; they will never let her go. For only she can save them before the Berserker curse destroys them all...

*

A dark fantasy romance... Mated to the Berserkers is a standalone, full length, MFM ménage romance starring two huge, dominant warriors who make it all about the woman.

TAKEN BY THE BERSERKERS - EXCERPT

The wolf stood in the center of the woodland path, lingering as if waiting for me. At first I didn't see the giant creature, mottled in shadow, with fur so black it looked almost blue. Once I did, I froze, clutching my baskets as if they could shield me. I could drop my wares and run, but if a predator of this size chased me, I was doomed.

After a good, hard glare in my direction, it slipped away, leaving me shaking with relief.

If I was wise, I'd return to the market and ask one of the villagers to escort me through the dangerous woods. Any one of the strapping young farm boys would be happy to see me home--my long, honey- blonde hair drew them like bees to nectar--but I preferred to make my way alone. My sisters and I lived at the end of the village, and I could be there before dark if no more wolves blocked my path.

A rustling in the brush told me there were more predators lurking, waiting for easy prey this close to dusk. I quickened my step and called to my sister Muriel as I drew close to our hut.

She met me on the stoop.

"Good market?"

I unslung my burden and handed her the empty baskets. "Enough to buy meat."

"Oh, Sabine, you didn't," Muriel said. "We have plenty from this month's offering."

I grunted, bending to enter the hut. I hadn't bought meat, even though I wanted to, because of the gift left on our doorstep, the gift we'd received each month since my sister Brenna had disappeared.

"How much do we have left?" I asked, waiting in the doorway until my eyes adjusted to the dank and smoke-filled space. Muriel moved by the fire, sorting the baskets and hanging up the bundles of leftover herbs.

"A whole hank. It was deer this time." Some months the meat was boar, or a slew of rabbits. It varied but it was always enough to fill our bellies for days, more if we salted and dried it. "I don't know why you don't like it."

"I'm grateful for the gift." The lie tasted bitter on my tongue. At one time, I believed the secret of Brenna's disappearance was tied to the gift of the meat. I'd waited up all night once, to try and catch the giver. Eventually, I'd fallen asleep. Just before dawn, I woke to the sound of a snapping twig. There on the ground, so close my foot could touch it, was a great boar carcass. The hunter had left it as I slept. It took all three of us to drag the beast to the firepit, and we carved it and ate on it for weeks. I never waited up to catch the the hunter again.

Muriel's voice shook me from my thoughts. "You don't have to eat it, you know. Fleur and I will eat our fair share, and give the rest away."

"Fleur should not be eating meat at all if she's still feeling ill. Just broth, and a little bit of oatcake." Youngest by a few minutes, the smaller twin took sick often. This evening, she huddled in a pile of blankets that made our bed in the corner of the hut.

I put away the herbs as Muriel pestered me with questions. "Who was at market? Did the priest bother you?"

"Nothing happened out of the ordinary. I saw a black wolf on the path coming home."

"An evil omen."

I shrugged. "No animal is truly evil. And wolves are often harbingers of good."

"Why didn't you ask one of the men from the village to walk you home? You know you could have any one of them."

I gave her a sharp look. Muriel, the eldest twin, looked far too knowing for her sixteen years.

"The men of the village are fools."

"Then how are you to marry one of them?"

"I won't. I will never marry. Love is foolish. It weakens the mind."

"What about us, then? I want to fall in love," Fleur asked in a weak voice.

I forced a smile for my two sisters. "And so you shall. You and Muriel will find your true love; I will make sure of it." I made my voice low and strong, mesmerizing as I wove the tale. "Strong men who will build you a house from the giant trees in the deep forest. They will carve your bed from a living tree and every child you bear will live."

"You don't want one then? A man?"

I bit my tongue against my true thoughts. Men were fools, too much trouble to handle. Half the time they acted like children, the other half raging brutes. I'd watched my mother fall for one who beat her and tried to grope my sister, who bore it silently, protecting us until she disappeared. My stepfather had been mauled by a beast soon after Brenna went missing. I'd laughed when I found his body.

"One man? I would never be satisfied. Perhaps two, if they were as brilliant as they were beautiful."

"Two men? At the same time?" Fleur wrinkled her nose.

"Why not?" I teased. "I can send them out together, to hunt and grunt and burp. I'll make them ask to be let back in my home."

Fleur laughed, but Muriel stayed quiet. When I puttered around the fire, she cornered me and spoke in a low voice.

"Only a few nights until full moon. Are you going to the grove?"

"Perhaps."

My sister sucked in a breath. "Be careful."

Instead of answering, I stooped and checked the unwanted meat. It came to our door fresh from the kill, bloody, as if ripped from the animal's body. Muriel roasted it with rosemary and other spices, and the smell made my mouth water. Scowling, I sliced some off for my supper.

At first I'd refused to eat the meat, as if rejecting the gift would bring my sister back. My mother had called me a fool.

"Your sister Brenna is dead," she had told me. "You have two younger sisters to care for. Any food is welcome."

I waited until my mother lay on her deathbed to tell her what I knew in my heart--somewhere, somehow, Brenna lived. I didn't know how I knew, but I did.

My mother had sighed. "Fey. Like your grandmother. She had a magic of the earth. It told her things; she knew they were true but could not explain why." My mother had clutched my hand with her wasted one. "Be careful, Sabine. Your grandmother's knowledge didn't save her when they burned her on a pyre."

"Sabine, did you hear me?" Muriel asked, bending her head close to mine so Fleur could not hear. "There's a dangerous beast about. It may be the wolf you saw. Father Benton went out one night for vespers and found all his goats slaughtered."

Last time Father Benton had spoken to me, he accused me of dallying with the devil. "How awful. The poor goats."

Muriel frowned at me. Dark-haired with grey eyes, she was growing into a beauty, but she had just as much wit, when her sweetness didn't stop her from using it. I kept her home as much as I could to keep the village men from noticing her. Some men were worse than wolves.

"I'll be careful, Muriel. You know as well as I, I need to go."

Tight-lipped, Muriel studied me for a moment before nodding. She understood.

I waited until she and Fleur had fallen asleep before slipping out of the hut in search of solitude.

Once a month, the heat came upon me. A curse from the goddess, my mother called it, though she didn't seem to suffer from it as intensely as I did. In my youth I would give in to the lust and find a man to sate the ache between my legs, but in the past few months I'd gone away alone, into the forest away from the village. The desire in me wasn't satisfied by a simple roll in the hay, it hungered for a man's strong arms, a tryst in a wild, secret place.

The moon rose and found me waist deep in the forest pool, wiping water on my fevered skin. I hummed a little as I swam.

I'd just left the pool and pulled on my gunna when I looked across the stream into the golden eyes of the wolf. My skirts tumbled into the water.

Foolish girl. I could hear my mother saying. *Out so late, alone.*

Slowly, I took a step back. The wolf stayed where it was. Another step, and another, and it seemed the beast would let me go. Muttering prayers to the goddess, I crept back the way I came.

I made it to the edge of the grove when I felt a wind at my back, a powerful pulse that sent shivers up my spine. Not daring to look back, I picked up my skirts and ran.

The lights of the hut danced in front of me. I burst onto the main path only to have strong arms like iron bands wrap around me.

My attacker pulled me backwards as I writhed and kicked. A hand slapped over my mouth. Panic choked in my throat. My legs thrashed the air as he dragged me back into the woods.

No, no, came my muffled shrieks as the trees crowded my vision. I lost sight of my family's hut. A few more steps and the light from the candle in the window disappeared in the gloom.

I kicked back at him as hard as I could, hoping to do some damage. The hand collaring my neck squeezed in warning.

"Sabine," the deep voice growled my name, and I went still with shock. "Be still."

"Please," I tried to beg, and when I couldn't get the word out, my arms and legs flailed in panic. The hand at my throat tightened, cutting off my scream. After few more kicks, the world receded and all went dark.

∼

I WOKE SORE, my body aching. My eyes still closed, I started to call to Muriel to check the chickens for eggs, and my throat screamed for water. Head pounding, I reached for the herbs I kept near our bed for Fleur's sickness. Nothing.

I opened my eyes. Instead of the hut, I lay on the ground of a great cave, wrapped in a fur robe. The morning air felt cool on my face. Had I lain outside all night?

Last night's terror came flooding back. The deep voice growling my name, the hand around my throat. As I glanced around the wide mouth of the cave and the wilderness beyond, I realized my nightmare was real.

Fear shot through me and I came to my feet, lunging for the forest. My escape was cut short when my leg pulled out from under me. I looked back and saw the chain around my ankle.

"No," I breathed, fingers wrenching at the heavy shackle. "No, no, no."

My attacker must have brought me to this cave in the wilderness and chained me as his prisoner. A wolf would gnaw off its foot to be free. I couldn't bring myself to do more than sit trembling on the ground.

I did not wait for long. My captor emerged from the woods, padding silently on bare feet. I rose, gripping the robe around me.

In the morning light his face was just as fearsome as last night, rawboned and cruel, sharp as a blade, rugged with stubble. He wore leather breeches but his feet and chest were bare. Twining over every inch of him--his arms, his hands, even his feet--were bluish tattoos, the markings of an ancient tribe far from Alba.

My heart pounded painfully as he walked closer, but he only carried his armful of firewood past me to a large fire pit surrounded by stones. When he rose, dusting his hands, his gaze met mine like a punch. My hands clenched into fists, but I refused to look away.

At last he reached down, picked up a bucket and brought it to me, setting it a few feet away--where I could reach it despite the chain.

"You must be thirsty," he rasped. "Drink."

I waited until he stepped back before forcing myself to walk forward and do as he'd ordered. The water tasted fresh. No poison, though if my captor wanted to kill me, he wouldn't have to resort to that. He stood like a warrior at the edge of battle, face blank and muscled body tensed as if ready to fight. The strength in his corded arms had dragged me forcibly from my doorstep. When I swallowed, I realized his grip had bruised my throat.

"Who are you?" I choked out. "Why am I here?"

"My name is Maddox." His voice sounded hoarse, as if he hadn't used it in many moons. Instead of answering my other question, he set his back to me and busied himself lighting a fire.

I drank another dipperful of water. My reflection looked frightened, so I schooled my features and drank slowly, glancing about for any way to escape.

"Don't try to run." Maddox said without looking up. "The woods are full of monsters." He angled his head and flashed me a smile that froze my blood. His canines looked rather sharp. "Or maybe I spread that rumor to keep everyone away."

I stood, needing the courage my height would give me. "If you don't want visitors, why am I here?"

Maddox stood and walked towards me with measured steps. My head tipped back as he loomed over me.

"You're not just a visitor." He stopped an arm's length

away. A head taller, and broader by half, he could easily overpower me. And he had. Instead of cowering, I tensed and gritted my teeth so I would stand my ground. If he wanted me here, he could deal with my defiance. If not, then I would die.

"What am I then?"

"A friend." His gaze fell to my chest, and I pulled the robe tighter so it covered the swell of my breast. Facing this tall, tattooed warrior with feral eyes, everything in me quivered.

He reached for me. I flinched, but let him brush a few golden hairs from my cheek. His face softened as his finger teased my hair.

"Friend?" I scoffed. "Do you chain up all your friends?"

His head canted to the side as he considered my question. Up close he smelled of smoke, the wild wood, and man.

Unable to keep still any longer, I stepped away. The clink of my chain seemed to rouse him.

He dropped his hand and walked towards the forest, tossing his answer over his shoulder. "Yes."

∼

NIGHT WAS FALLING when Maddox returned. I'd spent the day in the sun, as far away from the dark cave as I could. My chain wouldn't let me reach the fire, but I'd found a rock and beaten the chain with it, trying to find a weak point that would break my bonds. After midday, I'd become frantic, scratching at the rock that fixed the chain with my fingernails until they bled.

Finally, I sat on the rock, forcing myself to breathe deeply. I was a prisoner, but my captor didn't seem to have any malice against me. He even spoke to me. Perhaps I could reason with him.

With the rest of the water, I washed the blood from my hands and wiped my face. I combed my hair with my fingers and spent a long time braiding and rebraiding it. I would not panic. I was Sabine, considered the loveliest woman in the village, and a healer of ever increasing power. My herbs were sought after by noblemen and peasants alike. I could survive this.

That did not keep my heart from tripping wildly when Maddox walked out of the woods with his silent prowl. This time he carried a large buck slung over his shoulders. A beast of that size would be difficult for an ordinary man to carry, but Maddox walked without effort to the fire.

Throat dry, I watched the tattooed warrior gut the carcass and build a spit. His long knife tore through the flesh. The violence on top of my predicament sickened me, and I looked away.

"Do not fear, Sabine." I started at the sound of his voice. "I will not hurt you."

My hand went to my throat, sore from his bruising fingers. "You already have."

"It was necessary."

I walked to the end of my chain towards him to prove I wasn't afraid. "You could've left me alone."

His golden eyes pinned me suddenly. "I need you. "

"Why?"

"I need a healer."

I took a deep breath. "Then I will examine you."

"I'm not sick. Not yet." He speared a piece of meat with his knife and held it out to me. "Hungry?"

I was, but I didn't think I could swallow anything. My

hands fought not to close into fists at his glib answer. "Why don't you just let me go?"

He didn't answer, but kept slicing off bits of meat and catching them in a bowl. Finally he approached me and held it out. "Eat, little witch. You need your strength."

The scent of food made me even more hungry. And he was right. I needed fuel to plan my escape, but the victory in his expression when I took the bowl from him made me want to fling it back in his face. He'd given me the choicest parts of the meat, and because of my hunger, it seemed the best meal of my life. Maddox grinned, watching me devour the food.

"Good?" he grunted.

"Yes." I scowled. If he expected my thanks, he'd die waiting for it.

Forcing myself to eat slower, I took small sips from the bucket in between bites. My throat felt less sore. I almost wished it still hurt, as a reminder to me to hate my captor, instead of being intrigued by him. He'd choked me to unconsciousness. I should fear this warrior, but his deep voice and clear speech made him sound like a ruler, much more civilized than the rude surroundings.

Even his movements around the campfire were graceful, efficient. He'd set more wood nearby, where he could reach it and feed the fire into a roaring blaze that kept away the chill and the flies. For a rugged warrior, he seemed too smart by half, even if his speech was slow, stilted, as guttural as the growl of a wild creature.

The small pity I had for him made me angry. He wasn't the victim. I was. "What sort of man makes his home in a cave like a animal?"

I flinched when his shadow fell across me. But he only reached for my water bucket. "I think you know, Sabine." A tremor went through me at the sound of my name I still did not dare ask how he knew it.

"A barbarian?"

"An outcast."

When he returned with more water, my full stomach lent me courage.

"There must be a mistake. You cannot possibly mean to keep me here. What can I give you?"

He studied me as if working out what to tell me. "You are gift enough."

I tugged the bear pelt tighter around me. "What are you going to do with me?"

"Keep you safe, warm, fed."

"And chained." I shook my ankle.

"For now."

I quieted at this. No chain meant I could escape. I wondered what behavior would earn my freedom. Maddox smiled as if he knew my thoughts.

"So I am your pet," I snapped.

He didn't answer, just kept that cool smile as he built up the fire. I envisioned beating it from his face while I thought of a question that would not give him another chance to toy with me.

"I don't understand. I am but a simple village girl. I have nothing. I am nothing."

"You have magic."

"I do not--"

"Do not lie to me." His smile vanished. "I will not allow it."

"I am not lying. I grow herbs and make healing tonics. Whether they work or not is up to the goddess."

"You do not know your own power."

"You've made a mistake."

"Time will tell." Bending, he picked up the boulder securing my chain as if it were a mere pebble and carried it further into the cave.

"No." I grabbed the chain and pulled to no effect. "Please. Please do not make me go in there. I want to stay in the light."

Ignoring my pleas, Maddox carried the rock into the dry cavern, dragging me with it even though I struggled with all my might. In the end, I sat on the ground in the gloom, close to allowing myself to cry. This is what defying my captor bought me. He'd moved me only a few yards into the rocky shelter, but I would've rather remained outside in the elements. Without the sun on my face, my hope drained away.

"Do not be afraid, little witch. You are safe, for now." He started for the mouth of the cave.

"Wait," I rose to my feet, voice ringing in the enclosed space. "You're leaving?" My enemy was the closest friend I had in this place.

"It's safer for you if I am not here."

After he left, I sat mute near the fire, wringing my hands. My captor had not really hurt me, even though he seemed more a beast than man. Maybe I could survive this. I had to, not just for myself, then for Muriel and Fleur. They would be wondering what had happened to me, perhaps worrying over my fate, and their own. They were only two years younger, but I had always cared for them, kept them fed, kept them safe. What would happen to them if I was long gone? If--goddess forbid--I died in this place?

"I will not die," I muttered to myself. I would live to escape, and have my revenge on the smirking warrior who dragged me to this godforsaken place.

As the sun sank behind the trees, I explored as far as the

chain would allow. Deeper in the cave there was a sandy floor, leading to a pallet covered with a mound of old and reeking fur pelts. The musty stench filled the cave, lessened by the smoke of the fire. I went back to huddle as close as I could to the blaze, grateful for the fur robe Maddox had given me. That, at least, was clean.

As the moon rose, I prayed to the goddess to keep me and my sisters safe. The sounds of the forest filled my ears, including a call from the hills faraway, wild and lovely and achingly lonely.

I fell asleep to the howling of the wolves.

I woke during sunrise and stretched from my spot curled against the rock that kept me chained. Maddox had set the bucket near me, filled with fresh water. It wasn't until after I drank and washed my face that I realized I'd had another visitor in the night. Beside the rock, near the place where I'd slept, was a giant footprint, its span bigger than my head. Not man. Wolf.

TAKEN by the Berserkers is Sabine's story. Available now!

FREE BOOK

Get a secret Berserker book, Bred by the Berserkers (only to the awesomesauce fans on Lee's email list)
Go here to get started... https://geni.us/BredBerserker

WANT MORE BERSERKERS?

These fierce warriors will stop at nothing to claim their mates...

The Berserker Saga

Sold to the Berserkers - – Brenna, Samuel & Daegan
Mated to the Berserkers - – Brenna, Samuel & Daegan
Bred by the Berserkers (FREE novella only available at www.leesavino.com) - – Brenna, Samuel & Daegan
Taken by the Berserkers – Sabine, Ragnvald & Maddox
Given to the Berserkers – Muriel and her mates
Claimed by the Berserkers – Fleur and her mates

Berserker Brides

Rescued by the Berserker – Hazel & Knut
Captured by the Berserkers – Willow, Leif & Brokk
Kidnapped by the Berserkers – Sage, Thorbjorn & Rolf
Bonded to the Berserkers – Laurel, Haakon & Ulf

Berserker Babies – the sisters Brenna, Sabine, Muriel, Fleur and their mates
Night of the Berserkers – the witch Yseult's story
Owned by the Berserkers – Fern, Dagg & Svein
Tamed by the Berserkers — Sorrel, Thorsteinn & Vik
Mastered by the Berserkers — Juliet, Jarl & Fenrir

Berserker Warriors

Ægir *(formerly titled The Sea Wolf)*
Siebold

ALSO BY LEE SAVINO

Menage Romance

Draekons (Dragons in Exile) with Lili Zander (menage alien dragons)

Crashed spaceship. Prison planet. Two big, hulking, bronzed aliens who turn into dragons. The best part? The dragons insist I'm their mate.

Paranormal romance

Bad Boy Alphas with Renee Rose (bad boy werewolves)

Never ever date a werewolf.

Sci fi romance

Draekon Rebel Force with Lili Zander

Start with Draekon Warrior

Tsenturion Warriors with Golden Angel

Start with Alien Captive

Contemporary Romance

Royal Bad Boy

I'm not falling in love with my arrogant, annoying, sex god boss. Nope. No way.

Royally Fake Fiancé

The Duke of New Arcadia has an image problem only a fiancé can fix.

And I'm the lucky lady he's chosen to play Cinderella.

Beauty & The Lumberjacks

After this logging season, I'm giving up sex. For...reasons.

Her Marine Daddy

My hot Marine hero wants me to call him daddy...

Her Dueling Daddies

Two daddies are better than one.

Innocence: dark mafia romance with Stasia Black

I'm the king of the criminal underworld. I always get what I want. And she is my obsession.

Beauty's Beast: a dark romance with Stasia Black

Years ago, Daphne's father stole from me. Now it's time for her to pay her family's debt...with her body.

ABOUT THE AUTHOR

Lee Savino is a USA today bestselling author. She's also a mom and a choco-holic. She's written a bunch of books—all of them are "smexy" romance. Smexy, as in "smart and sexy."

She hopes you liked this book.

Find her at:
www.leesavino.com

Text copyright © 2016 Lee Savino
All Rights Reserved

No part of this book may be reproduced in any form or by any electronic or mechanical means including information storage and retrieval systems, without permission in writing from the author. The only exception is by a reviewer, who may quote short excerpts in a review.

This book is a work of fiction. Names, characters, places, and incidents either are products of the author's imagination or are used fictitiously. Any resemblance to actual persons, living or dead, events, or locales is entirely coincidental.

Printed in Great Britain
by Amazon